LAST OF A DYING BREED 2

Lock Down Publications and Ca$h
Presents
Last of a Dying Breed 2
A Novel by *Jamaica*

Lock Down Publications
P.O. Box 944
Stockbridge, Ga 30281
www.lockdownpublications.com

Copyright 2021 by Jamaica
Last of a Dying Breed 2

First Edition January 2021
Printed in the United States of America

Lock Down Publications
Like our page on Facebook: Lock Down Publications @
www.facebook.com/lockdownpublications.ldp
Cover design and layout by: **Dynasty Cover Me**
Book interior design by: **Shawn Walker**
Edited by: **Shawn Walker**

Stay Connected with Us!

Text **LOCKDOWN** to 22828 to stay up-to-date with new releases, sneak peaks, contests and more…

Thank you!

Submission Guideline.

Submit the first three chapters of your completed manuscript
to ldpsubmissions@gmail.com, subject line: Your book's title. The
manuscript must be in a .doc file and sent as an attachment.
Document should be in Times New Roman, double spaced and in
size 12 font. Also, provide your synopsis and full contact
information. If sending multiple submissions, they must each be in
a separate email.

Have a story but no way to send it electronically? You can still
submit to LDP/Ca$h Presents. Send in the first three chapters,
written or typed, of your completed manuscript to:

LDP: Submissions Dept
P.O. Box 944
Stockbridge, Ga 30281

DO NOT send original manuscript. Must be a duplicate.

Provide your synopsis and a cover letter containing your full
contact information.

Thanks for considering LDP and Ca$h Presents.

Acknowledgement

Lord, thank you for your grace, mercy and unconditional love. Lord, I owe you for holding me together when I had every reason to fall apart.

To my Kids, My Family and MY down ass friends, THANK YOU.

My Fans, I don't know where I would be if it wasn't for y'all, the LOVE and SUPPORT is definitely REAL and TRUE.

To my TEAM, LOCK DOWN PUBLICATIONS, the game is OURS!

Jeezy and Boosie, thank you. I don't know what I would do without the bangers from y'all.

To all MY people that's LOCKED up, hold ya head, and stay grounded, but most of all, stay prayed UP.

I didn't mention any names this time, but FR, I got each and every one next time!!!

FB: Tha Author Jamaica
IG: Tha_author_jamaica
Snap: Tha Author Jamaica
Or Julianj9815

Email: 1720jamaica@gmail.com

Dedication

To MYSELF
Artist: Jeezy
Song: Get YA Mind Right

I'll NEVER trust another, it's only one person who is going to keep it realer than real and that's myself. WE are living in a time where your friend will kill you and hug your mother at your funeral. People won't love you until you are dead and gone. If your loyalty change cause you are mad, YOU was never loyal. YOUR words only prove who you want to be but YOUR actions prove who you really are. If I rocks with you, you gonna feel, know and see it and IF I don't, you definitely gonna feel that too.

Before I bounce, let me say this last thing--- Why is it that niggas get mad when they snitch and you call them out on it. They wanna fight, but didn't want to fight the case. SMDH... The whole HOOD could have a niggas paper work but IF his BAG is right, it's like he never snitch. A snitch is a SNITCH, no matter how you look at it. But when LOYALTY, RESPECT and MORALS come back in style, all y'all succas in trouble!!! LOYALTY is MORE than a WORD. IT'S a WAY of LIFE!!! So show, live and die bout it!!!

Chapter 1

Love

"What the fuck you said in that letter?" I questioned Murda the second our call was linked together.

"Love, it ain't what you think."

His statement triggered me to laugh out loud in his ear. "It ain't what I think?" I rubbed my hands together. "But you took the time to ink me that fuck shit rather than tell me that fuckery over the phone like the real nigga you declare to be." I dropped my head feeling defeated. "But it ain't what I think." I stopped to catch my breath and control my feelings that was on full display.

"You talk to me every muthafuckin' day, yo" I was heated, hotter than a Mac 11 with a hunnid round clip. "Hello?" I snapped. I was tired of just hearing him breathing. Cat had this nigga's tongue. "Murda, talk to me," my legs were shaking uncontrollably, as the police officer walked around the unit on the top tier doing his rounds.

"Mane, that shit wasn't supposed to happen, Love."

"It wasn't supposed to be like that," I chuckled as white dots appeared in my vision. My blood pressure was all the way up with the words that he was spitting to me. "But you the nigga that got," I cut short my words as I mentally replayed the words on paper that I received from him.

Dear Love,

...You always preached to me, "Tell me before someone else does." Well, I have a baby on the way...

"A bitch pregnant?" I shut my eyes, unable to fully process the words from his letter.

...Mane, I know you said I could fuck anyone, just as long as I don't get anyone pregnant, and I did. That shit fucks with me every day since I found out that Kandi is having a baby, Love. I am fucking shedding tears from my soul as I write you this fucked up shit. I

don't know what to do or what to say for you to forgive me. But I know one thing for sure. I'm muthafuckin' sorry.
I love you Love, always and forever.
Murda

"Love," he said my name and everything I ate earlier felt like it was coming back up.

"Loyalty over everythin', you know that right?"

He didn't say a word, so before I kept going, I wiped the tears away from my face feeling my heart beating three times harder and faster. "From here on, let me do my time and let me do it in peace."

"Love…"

"Don't put my fuckin' name in ya mouth." I cut him off, my tone was low but filled with resentment. "You weren't thinking 'bout me when you were busting in that bitch!" I spazzed out. "You're dead to me!"

"Love," he voiced, but I cut him off again.

"Don't do shit else for my seeds!"

"Really yo?" he barked, and I could hear the hurt in his voice.

It was my time to let the fire burn. *An eye for an eye.* I wasn't going to be the only one hurting. "Yea, you heard me. You are dead to me. And when I don't fuck with you, I don't need you to fuck with my seeds!" I slammed the phone in his ear. I knew how much he loved my kids, so not being able to do shit for them or see them would hurt him the most.

"Lock Down!" The officer screamed as I walked away from the phone with my head up, as the tears splashed from my eyes. Aliceville fucking Alabama. That's where I was at for the moment, and I couldn't wait for my paperwork to go through so I could get the fuck away from here. I needed a fresh start.

"Lock Down!" The young officer yelled again, and this time I just stared him down as he approached my room, daring him to lock me the fuck out. Tonight, was the night that they were going to see me act a fucking fool. Inmate or not.

"Ms. Jenkins, really?" He locked room 217's door.

"I know you see me walking." I lived in 215.

"Don't make me…" he started to say.

"Don't make me write an incident report?" I stopped at my room with my hand on the handle. "Is that what you threatening me with?" I questioned him when he didn't answer my first question.

"Get in your room!"

Just like the fuck I thought, this nigga wasn't 'bout that life. I called his bluff and he ain't said shit.

"Without that badge, you are a bitch and a half," I sang that Boosie joint out loud.

I jerked the door open and closed it behind me quietly realizing that my celly was knocked the fuck out.

Click. Clack.

The keys turned and for a quick moment, I wanted to turn around and kick that muthafuckin' door, but he was saved by my celly. I showed respect 'cause I expected nothing less.

"Ughhhhhhh," I cuffed my mouth with both of my hands, trying to hold the hurt and pain in that I was feeling at the moment from fucking with Murda.

"Count time!"

I was so ready for this bid to be over with. I could feel freedom already with only four years into my fifteen-year sentence. All those muthafuckas that stunted on me since I had been caged up, had it coming. Murda had added himself to my shit list, thanks to his dick.

Yes, he held me down when I needed him the most, but I had made it clear that he wasn't to get anyone pregnant. Fuck the world but strap up! I knew he had needs, but damn, *was the nigga in love, too?* I wondered.

"Bunkie," I rubbed her leg. "Get up, it's count time," she pulled the covers from her body revealing her light color gray sweats as she sat up.

"Thank you," she said.

My tears had dried up, but my feelings were still crushed. My heart was broken into pieces. My mind was wondering as my body shook, not from the cold air from the vent but from hurt. *I was always getting hurt dealing with niggas.*

"Are you okay?" My celly asked me as I rocked back and forth, standing up. Nigga had me fucked all the way up. "Are you okay?" She asked me again when I didn't answer.

"Yes," I lied. "I'm good." I whispered as we watched the two officers pass our room. As soon as they were out of sight, I climbed on the ladder and up into my bed, I went. Fuck waiting on them to yell, "Count Clear!"

"Night, night Love. Whatever it is, it is going to be okay." Ms. Kanell said.

"Good night." I said, rolling over to face the wall as tears graced my pillowcase.

Midnight

I didn't know how long it had taken me to fall asleep, but I woke up exactly at twelve a.m. according to my G-shock watch. A light snore from under me let me know that my bunkie was sleeping.

I grabbed my book light from the rails on my bed and pinned it to my gray long-sleeved shirt. I was up, my heart and soul were mad heavy from adversity that Murda had caused and I had to let him know exactly how the fuck I was carrying this fuckery with him.

I lifted the bottom of my bed up slowly trying not to stir my celly as I reached for my blue ink pen and some paper from under my mat, only to grab one of Murda's old letters that he had inked me. I positioned myself as I traveled back down memory lane to his joint.

Love,

Conspiracy catches more play than Drake's new shit on the radio and the little journey that you on ain't nothing but a minor setback for a major come back. Loyalty builds an empire, and our foundation is set on respect. Can't nothing destroy us, let alone scratch our armor.

Yo, what's good? How are you doing? I'm peace, just thought of you so I decided to put pen to paper and give us both something to do because truth be told, I miss the fuck out of you! The babies are good! The business is doing ok! Shit is just crazy out here, especially since you ain't here with me.

I heard about all these new drugs laws, so you know I got my fingers crossed, right? It's been 4 years 3 months and 10 days since you been gone. I can't believe you are on the other side of the country, but don't trip, I'ma find a way to visit you!

The picture we got together is perfect, the government wanted to destroy our love, but they only made it stronger. I love the 10-page letter you wrote me, it surprised me 'cause it was so real and raw, and hell yeah the Feds Ain't Watching 'Cause These Succas Telling.

I got an interview with Coffee to tell ya story, and I'm glad that I can put a curve to your lips (smile). You know I only got a soft spot for you, nobody else! We picture perfect, remember that.

Silence is golden, and a lion ain't gotta roar for people to know it's a lion. I know what you stand for and best believe me the streets do, too. I've learned a long time ago that a man is only as great as the woman who stands beside him, whether it be platonic or much more because like-minded individuals build empires!

It's a must that you stay strong and focus to win this battle, 'cause two things you have left to count on is the undivided love that ya seeds and I have for you!

I see you fucking with Jeezy and Booise hard as hell (lol) as long as them niggas know that I come first. (Smile) Oh yeah, I don't give a fuck how old I am gonna be when you touch down, I want two more babies, and I want them from you!

You know how desperate these bitches are. Literally. I throw them a bottle of water and a three-pack condom box 'cause I know they are thirsty. And I don't want something only Magic Johnson's got money to get rid of.

I'ma beat my dick for 15 years, shit Papoose did it for Remy Ma for 7! I got this, boo! I know what kind of woman I have, and I refuse to fuck it up over some pussy! Can't nan bitch compare to you, so why am I gonna look? I don't move backwards.

Yo, it's late so I'll end this for now but not forever and until pen meets paper, I'll be thinking/missing/loving you!

You Already Know,

Murda

Pussy ass nigga sold me a dream and I fell for it. Even though my mom had been dead for years, her words still played over and over in my head. *"No matter what happens, promise me that you'll take care of yourself. Never settle for less! Never let a man belittle or take advantage of you!"*

Her words and my anger added more fuel to the fire. I powered up my MP3 player and got to work.

Murda,
Artist: Jeezy
Song: Get Ya Mind Right

Dead or Alive, I'ma be #1. Was ya #1, realer than any bitch you've ever fucked with. But you fucked that shit up. I've been rock-steady to you, so you already know I'm not 'bout to settle for anything that I wouldn't settle for when I was free.

And I damn sure not about to kiss ya ass 'cause I'm caged up. Fuck outta here!

You right, I'm on a journey, it's nothing but a minor setback for a major come back. I thought loyalty had our foundation frozen, but you allowed pussy to fuck up our empire. Our armor is zipped up in a body bag-dead!

I don't even know who the fuck you are. I str8 up told you from jump that you could fuck the world, just don't get anyone pregnant, but you stayed preaching how you was good and why would you do something like that when you had a Queen in your life? Which face were you showing me then? Now, I am 'bout to carry you like I drag every other muthafucka that betrayed me. Real Talk. Know this, they can't hold a real bitch forever! Dead or alive, I'm coming out this bitch, nigga. You lost a bitch that was a solid keeper, now you are dead to me. Dead to US. My kids, too, pussy ass nigga. This shit ain't nothing but rain drops, been in storms all my life and you should already know how I carried those. I'm stamped as the realest bitch to ever did it.

Last of A Dying Breed,

Muthafuckin' Ms. Love Jenkins

I folded the letter and placed it into an envelope as the officers did their 12 a.m. count even though it was 12:30 a.m.

My mind ran widely. I should have never shown love to a lot of niggas, but the thorough bitch that I was, did. There was no reason to cry about it now. I'd been a stack from the womb, and I'll die loyal to the soil.

The nigga that raped me, the pussy that snitched on me, hurt me, no one! There wasn't a man alive that was capable of breaking me, not even Murda.

"Fuck those pussy ass niggas," I said, as I laid my head to rest. *God forgives, but I won't forget.*

Chapter 2

Murda

The moment Love hung the phone up in my ear, I knew that any love that she had for me was over and done with. Every single word she spat at me damaged every fiber in my body. My heart shattered into a million pieces when she said, *You're dead to me. And when I don't fuck with you, I don't need you to fuck with my seeds.* "Fuck!" A bellow of pain escaped from my soul. Never in my life time did I want to hurt Love, or destroy her spirit, but I allowed lust and my dick to think for me instead of my heart, for once.

Five years had gone by and I was faithful to the core to Love, until Kandi, my last baby ma, the bitch that I married, caught me slippin' and I felt for her.

"Damn," I dropped my head in my hands as I relieved the moment that was causing me all this heartache.

"Murda, I'm telling you, Marley stay acting the fuck out in school," she preached to me over the phone.

"All right, I'ma take a trip up there this weekend and holla at him, Kandi."

"You've been saying that shit forever, but you never made it up here!" She screamed and I couldn't even debate with her because her words were the truth. "You think money can fix everything, Murda?" she continued with her voice way lower than before.

"All I'm asking you is to help me raise our son, that's it, nothing more." The urgency in her voice let me know that shit was serious.

I tried my hardest to visit my son, Marley, every three months even though we Facetimed every week. I made sure my week was clear, so I asked my right-hand man, Smoke, to hold shit down for me while I was away and he agreed without a question. I informed Love about the trip, like I've always done and she was cool. When it came down to my kids, baby girl always had my back a hundred percent.

I drove seven and a half hours nonstop, unless I had to fuel up. It was 3 a.m. when I reached my destination in Brooklyn, New York. Ding. Dong. I pushed the button rubbing my eyes. When minutes passed and she didn't answer, I decided to call her phone.

"Hello," she answered in a sleepy voice.

"You gonna let me in or not, yo?"

"Huh?" She expressed, probably confused and shocked all in one.

"I'm at ya door!" I dropped the phone call and hit the button again. Not too long, then the bolts unlocking. The moment the door cracked open; I inhaled her scent. Baby Powder.

"You have a nigga in here?" I always asked before I stepped into her crib.

"And you think that I would open this bitch up if I had one up in here?" Was always her answer. Her mouth was vicious, just like her actions. I moved past her only to sink in her scent even more. At one-point, Kandi had me gone, she had my heart at her feet until she fucked my worst enemy, the nigga that killed my homie, Pop.

"I stay asking 'cuz I'm not 'bout to beef over some pussy that ain't mine." I moved towards the bathroom, leaving her at the door.

I knew my way around the crib, freely. I was the one that picked the apartment out for us, back then when we were a couple. Nothing major changed with the decoration in the crib at all.

I closed my eyes as I released my bladder. "Damn!" I'd been holding my piss for hours. I handled my business, then I searched the cabinet to see if there were any men hygiene laying around. Not that I cared, I didn't want to get caught slipping in her crib knowing what she had done back in the day. I found none as always. Kandi stayed saying, "I don't have no man, but Marley!" I found it hard to believe because she was pretty.

I found Kandi in the kitchen getting something to drink. "You want something to drink, B?" Her New York accent was strong as fuck. She was a high yellow bone, Brooklyn born and raised diva. Standing at 5 feet 7inches, she had it going on but her attitude, quick temper made her unattractive to me.

"*Yea, what do you have to drink?*" *I asked, pulling a chair out from at the table so I could sit down and email Love on my Corrlinks account that I had set up for us to communicate.*

"*Anything you want,*" *she leaned her body against the counter, arching her back, as her head tilted to one side with a devilish smile on her face.*

"*It ain't that type of party, shorty.*" *Her body was still in tack. She was solid and thick in all the right places. Her tights were glued to her body like concrete did to cinder blocks. Her shirt stopped right at her waist, exposing her belly button ring. Her hair was wrapped up under her scarf as her piercings showed on her face. One above her left eye and the other in the crease of her lips on the right-hand side.*

"*Whatever, Murda, I ain't said shit out the way, son,*" *she laughed as she turned her body around tipping on her toes to get me a glass from the cabinet. I watched her ass cheeks clapped and I couldn't do shit but shake my fucking head from side to side.*

"*Matter of a fact,*" *she caught me checking her out,* "*you know ya way around.*" *She sat the glass on the table,* "*help ya own self!*" *And with that she bounced.*

Thank God.

I logged into my account so I could update my baby about what was happening.

Baby,

It's 3:30 a.m. and I'm finally in NY. I'm tired AF, but I'm good. Can't wait to wake my soldier up in the morning and see his reaction. How was your day? I hope everything is peaceful on your end. I love you.

Love,

Ya RN4L

I hit send and tucked my phone into my pocket before I got up and grabbed me a bottle of water from the fridge. I gulped that shit down as I crushed a bag of potato chips in seconds.

"Fuck!" I said in a whisper as I walked to my son's room. His door was halfway cracked open. His dragon night light was plugged into the wall across the room. I removed my Timbs at the door checking out all the photos posted up around his room. My favorite one was the day he was born, and I held him for the first time in the delivery room.

Marley was so small that he rested right in my palm. He was a premature baby, weighing 3 pounds 7ounces. Kandi went into labor at 5 and a ½ months. I thought Marley wasn't going to make it, but my soldier pulled through. I spent nights at the hospital as he grew in the incubator.

Now my little goon was seven and a mirror of my reflection. When he was born, I claimed him, but when I found out Kandi fucked that nigga, Shook, from another bitch that tried to give me the pussy, I got a paternity test done. I was the father.

I wanted to wake him up, but I knew if I did, we'd be up all night, so I grabbed a pillow from his bed and took a spot on the carpet.

The early morning sound from Marley's voice touched my soul as I opened up my eyes. "Daddy!" He hugged my neck with all his strength.

"Aww, G," I welcomed his embrace. "Good morning, my G."

"Daddy!" He hollered again and hearing his voice, in person, touched my heart. My kids were my everything and more, all nine of them.

"Come on, little man, let's get you ready for school."

"Aww, mane, do I have to go today?" I watched sadness wash all over his face.

"Yea, why not?"

"Cause," he dropped his head, "you not going to be here when I get home."

"I am for a few days." I announced, as his face lit up like a Christmas tree.

"Yes," he screamed, bouncing around the room.

***

I dropped him off at school and was there to pick him up.
"Where's Mommie?" he asked, getting into the rental.
"At work." Kandi had gone back to school and got her CNA
license and she made use of it.
"Do I still have to go to grandma's house, Dad?" Kandi's mom
kept him once school was over until she got off from work at six.
"Naw, it's just us." I rubbed his head as he took the shotgun
spot. I took my little one around the city as we listened to Jay Z.
Nothing in the world mattered to me at the moment but this time that
we were sharing. After spending nearly the entire evening out, we
decided to stop at the store and grab some groceries since Marley
wanted to surprise his mom with dinner. We spent almost an hour
in Wegmans. "You have everything that you need, son?" I chuckled
as we waited in line. My little King had picked up almost the entire
store.
"I think I picked up everything that we need, Dad." He looked
up at me and smiled. Our total came out to be a few hundred,
nothing that I couldn't spare.
I loaded the trunk up as I rapped to Smoke about the Burg and
how things were moving. "Same shit different day," he informed
me.
Our conversation was cut short as I entered the driver side. I
kept that street shit out of my son's ears.
Two hours later dinner was ready with a lot of my help, but the
time that me and Marley shared was worth it all.
"Awww," Kandi screamed, wrapping her hands around our
son the moment he told her that he had made her dinner.
"Mom," he whined, trying to move his body out of her embrace.
"What you don't want ya daddy to know that you're a momma's
boy?" she laughed and I couldn't help but to smile.

I could tell that my baby ma was happy that I had taken the time to make this trip. It was written all over her face. It was a peace that I couldn't describe. I hadn't seen that in a very long time.

After dinner, I spent the rest of the evening with my seed.

"You have to be the man of the house and you can't afford to stress ya mom out." I kept shit real with my kids, no shades, everything straight forward. "You have to treat her right and that means with respect."

"You have to listen to Mommie because she wants the very best for you." Marley nodded his head. "Make us proud."

Noticing the time, I paused the game and instructed him to brush his teeth.

"Yes, Daddy."

Moments later, after he had done everything, I tucked him in. "I'll be back here soon." It was my last night.

"Daddy, you promise?" He began tearing up.

"My word." I hugged him tightly. "I promise, my word is all that I have and remember what I told you?"

"Yes. My word is all I have in this world."

"Okay, good. I love you!" After hugging him for a time, I let him go so he could see my face.

"I love you too, Daddy." And down his tears came. It broke my heart to see him so crushed. Fuck.

My time in NY was well spent and drama free. Kandi wasn't on no fuckery until it was time for me to bounce.

"I don't understand how you can love a bitch that's got a 15 years sentence, Murda." We were sitting at the kitchen table sipping on a bottle of Ciroc. She knew all about Love 'cause I told her what the deal was.

"I have a woman and yes, she's locked up, but I am waiting on her."

"How, Murda?" Pain echoed from her tone. I knew Kandi wanted me back but I couldn't travel that road again, especially after all that had happened. No matter how many times I told her it was over, she kept that little bit of hope dwelled inside of her.

"Location doesn't change the love that you have for someone, shorty."

"I can't tell." Her words slurred from her mouth, considering she had more than just a sip. "Murda," she leaned her head back and I couldn't help but to look at my name still tatted on her chest, her heart. "I'm sorry. I'm so fucking sorry. I know I fucked up and I need you to forgive me!" She looked me dead in my eyes. "I wish I could take it back, Martin," she called me by my birth name. "I swear, I am so sorry!" she cried.

I got up to leave 'cause I didn't want to relive the pain I went through when I found out she fucked that pussy.

"I'ma swing back up here next month," I said, dropping about five bands on the table.

"Murda," she pushed the money away, grabbing a hold of my hand. "I'm sorry." Her touch made me freeze, her scent had me in a daze and before I knew what was happening, Kandi was on her knees, my back was against the wall and my dick was deep down in her mouth. That shit happened so fast that I didn't even push her off me.

The noise that she made with my dick in her mouth had me grabbing the back of her head as I rocked all the way up inside her jaw. It had been years since I had some skin on my dick.

"Damn!" I held her head, pulling her scarf off, watching her hair fall all the way down from her wrap. When she glanced up at me with her tongue ring sliding back and forth on the tip of my dick, I thought I could handle her and push her off me, but my dick wanted this.

"Got damn!" My legs wobbled. I grabbed a handful of her hair, trying to pull her up off her knees, but when our eyes locked, I realized that it was way too late for me to quit. The damage was already done.

There was no way I was going to tell Love. I had to bury this secret with me, fuck confessing this to Love. I dropped Love to the back of my mind as I focused my attention to the brain hawk in front of me.

When Kandi started touching herself, my body jerked forward on my toes. "Fuck!" I voiced, pulling her hair from the root, guiding her up to my body.

"Why the fuck you do that shit for, Murda?" She licked her lips from side to side. There was no need to respond to her. I lead Kandi, my wife by law, still, because she never signed the divorced papers to her bedroom.

"Murda," she sang in a sexy tone as I laid her on her stomach at the end of the bed. "Murda," she purred, and I ripped her big T-shirt off, pulling her panties to the side and dropping my pants at my feet, not taking my Timberlands off.

I watched our shadows across the room on the wall from the light bouncing off of the TV.

She pushed her ass up into the air as I spread her ass cheeks, showing me the sun, the moon and all of the above.

"Got damn!" I eased my dick up into her. Her pussy felt so much better than my palm and Vaseline did. "Damn, I need a condom," I said, but when she lifted her right leg up, my breathing stopped as she tossed her ass back to me. I gripped her waist, listening to the noise our body was creating forgetting all about the condom.

She twerked her ass round and round in circles with my dick deep inside of her.

"Fuck me, Murda! Fuck me!" She screamed with her head stuffed into the bed. And I did just that, long deep strokes with my hands gripping her waist.

"Ughhhhhh," she screamed out into pure bliss. With each motion that I thrust inside of her I knew that she wasn't touched by anyone, her pussy was tight as fuck. "Murda," she sang my name and it drove me over the edge. I fucked her till I got soft and hard again.

***

"Fuck!" I kicked the table, picking up the bottle of Henny and smashing it against the wall. Reliving that night that costed me my future with Love, had me ready to drive to Brooklyn, New York and smoke Kandi's ass myself, like I should have done from the start, when I found out that she fucked that pussy ass nigga.

"Bruh," Smoke voiced as he watched me let my pain and frustration out. "I fucked up!" The base in my voice rocked my body forward, knocking me into the wall. It took everything I had in my body to get myself together. "My bad, bruh," I said, pointing to the little destruction that I had caused in his spot.

"It's all good, fam," he replied, "I know how you feel. She'll come around, just give her some time."

But I knew better, Love held grudges forever, and once you crossed her, it was a wrap.

"I hope so," I said, pulling the hoodie over my head and resting my hand on my heater.

As I bounced from his crib. I needed to be alone to get my thoughts together.

It was way past midnight, and I had been sitting for almost two hours waiting for the pussy ass nigga, Slim, to leave his mom's spot on Park Ave. Fool had been ducking me for about two weeks now, not answering any of my calls.

"Boss man, give me two days," he said when I fronted him the pound of hydro.

"Bet."

Two days turned into three, three turned into a week and here it was two weeks later and still nothing from ol'boy. Niggas thought the streets was a game, but I didn't. It was trap or die out in this bitch for me. Muthafuckas claimed they were real, but they were not me, so I had to show them real.

I watched Slim exit his mom's spot not even paying attention to his surroundings. He had that happy walk strutting like he didn't owe me some bread. It's not always 'bout that bread with me, principles and morals saved a lot of nigga's lives.

Slim could've called me and explained his situation, but to duck me for as long as he did, was a problem.

As soon as he pulled off, I did, too.

The Burg had been slow as fuck for the past few days due to the indictments that had come out, so traffic was mad weak. Niggas disappeared off the map, staying out of sight until shit was clear, but not me. I was on my grind, fuck the pigs, if them muthafuckaz wanted me, they better come correct.

After about ten minutes of driving, Slim was at his spot in Rivermont. I hit my lights and parked about six cars back, leaving my engine running, before he even parked.

My feet dashed across the concrete as my eyes glanced around the block searching for anything out the way.

"Slim," I greeted him as he closed his door. His body jumped, as his eyes popped up like a fresh batch of popcorn. He was shocked as hell to see me.

"What's good, fam?" He tried to dap me up, but I pushed the nine into his chest.

"Naw." I refused his hand.

"It ain't like that," he held his hands up in the air, feeling the tension. "I was gonna get with you in the morning. Fam, you know it's not like…

Blocka!

Blocka!

Blocka!

His body hit the car.

Blocka!

Blocka!

His entire body slid down the car.

I dashed back to my ride feeling a little bit more relief. That nigga created an enemy when I'd been solid to him. He crossed that line so I left him flat lined.

Chapter 3

Murdoc

Shit is so fucked up, that I can't even seem to figure out how I made it this far, without being toe tagged by someone, especially Love. No matter how hard I knocked her down, that bitch had a way of bouncing back like cooked crack, fresh out of the pot. Yes, I knew there was no chance with me getting her back, but it's worth a try and she was worth it all. Fuck that nigga that she's rocking with, I am her kids' father, the one and only.

Seeing a pillow flying across the room, I screamed. "What the fuck, yo?" I screamed at Shorty for breaking my train of thought. "What?" I snapped, since she just wanted to stand and stare.

"Why the fuck you treating me like this?" She whined with her hands on her hips.

Nothing that bitch said moved me, not even her teardrops. She was nothing more than just a fuck, nothing more, but everything less.

"Murdoc," she paused and I waited for the stupid shit that was about to be released from her mouth. "I hate how you treat me when you know how I'm feeling 'bout you."

"Feeling about me?" I laughed so hard that I had to hold my stomach. "Cut that shit out, yo," I got up from the bed as I reached for my boxers on the floor. We had just fucked.

"You ain't shit!" She started to walk towards the bed, and I knew from her tone, I had to put my hands on her just for her to understand that I wasn't a fucking game. I hated when females ran their mouths at me in a reckless manner.

"Oh, I ain't shit?" I slipped into my boxers as I kept my eyes on this dumb bitch approaching with an *I wanna fight you attitude.*

"Tamaine, I can't believe you," she pointed her finger in my face.

"Bitch!" I snapped, bending her finger to the back.

"Oh, my gawwwwwd!" She hollered out in pain.

"What the fuck I told you 'bout ya muthafuckin' fingers, bitch?" I took that muthafucka further back, watching tears roll down her cheeks, as her knees buckled. "What the fuck I told you?" Her left hand grabbed my hand but the hold that I had on her fingers made her body weak. "Oh, you not gonna answer me?" Her stupidity had brought this up on her, I have told her on several occasions about her tone and her muthafuckin' fingers. "Don't raise your voice when you talk to me and keep your body parts to yourself."

But that shit went in one ear and out the other. Bitches could not appreciate when I was calm, cool and collected, they wanted to make me into a monster and since that's what she wanted, I was giving it to her.

"Keep my hands to myself," she hollered out in pain as the tears poured down her face at a rapid pace.

"So why the fuck you had them on me?"

"I'm sorry," she screamed, trying to find a way to ease the pressure from her finger. "I'm so, so, so sorry. It won't happen again," she pleaded.

Watching the pain flash across her face, I let her hand go hearing the sorry in her voice.

"Next time you do that shit, I'ma break all ten of them. Now get ya shit and get the fuck outta my crib," I said, stepping over her. "Make that shit quick, yo!" I treated that hoe how she wanted me to treat her, like a real dumb one.

Shortly after shorty was gone, I gathered a few things to make a move. Yes, I was still in the game, still hustling drugs. The streets were my home, that's all I knew from a young age. I taught Love, everything she knew, but in the end, she turned out to be a better beast than me and most niggas. It took me a very long time to admit that, but it was straight facts. Niggas had more respect for Love than they did for most niggas, dead or alive. She was the best thing that I ever had till I lost her.

I treated her so fucking bad, and it's a sad 'cause I was her first love, but I know deep down, that I will always be her only true love.

And that was my motivation. I was on a mission to get her back with my kids so we can be a family, plus the little girl that I had on her. "Murdoc?" the fiend hollered out my name the second I got out my ride, "Murdoc, let me holla at you. I got all the money this time." The old man, Pusha said, walking to me with a limp.

"What the fuck happened to you?" I questioned him reaching into my pocket to get the extra work that I had to serve the fiends.

"Fucking Mary ran me over with the car," he said with a smile on his face, but I didn't find shit funny about someone getting hit by a car. I had been in a few accidents and them muthafuckas scared me. I loved my life.

"What?" I leaned on the Audi.

"She came home hollering how she heard I was fucking Michelle," he said, laughing now.

"Michelle?" I questioned him wanting to know who the hell he was talking 'bout.

"Michelle with the big ol ass, with the missing teeth," he tilted his head from side to side as I listened to the story that had him all cracked up. I didn't know the Michelle he was talking about, but I listened closely.

"So, I am telling Mary, that shit is not true, I was just with her to get my high on, nothing more," he started to look around. "But she didn't believe me, so I walked out the house 'cause I didn't want to cause a scene in front of our grandkids." He stopped talking for another second before he continued, "so I'm walking down the road not thinking about anything but getting high 'cause Mary done went back in the house. But then I heard the car tires before it hit me. I tried to jump out the way, but I wasn't fast enough. That woman was crazy so I expected that from her, but this time she almost killed me," he held his side. "Murdoc," he pulled a fifty out his pocket, "give me a forty, I owed you ten from last time. And all I want to do right now, is chill and get high."

I reached into my pocket and grabbed three twenty pieces, as I looked around making sure no one was looking and making sure I didn't see any pigs in sight. "It's all good, Pusha," I placed the pieces in his hand, "that extra is for your pain," I collected my money from him.

"Nuff love, Murdoc. You know if I was high, I probably would have been able to jump over the car that night Mary hit me." We both cracked the fuck up before he walked off 'cause we both knew that shit was true.

Drugs gave that extra strength that was needed. It didn't matter if it was day or night, rain, sleet or snow, I knew first hand. Drugs had a nigga doing real stupid shit.

I recalled one night, I was on that PCP also known as *Wet* on Federal Street, and I had taken all my clothes off. I heard the next day when my high had worn down, how Love came through and saw me all fucked up.

"Bruh, ya baby ma, Love, dropped her head seeing you all fucked up, fam," my little nigga, Pac, told me. "You could tell that she wanted to cry but somehow, she pulled herself together and bounced."

How the fuck am I going to get her back? I questioned myself as I walked into the store.

"Yo!" I greeted the Arab that was around the counter.

"You tell me, Murdoc?"

I had been coming here since I was kid, and into the streets, this joint was the neighborhood spot. They supplied everything anyone wanted and if they didn't have it, they made sure to get it for their customers.

"Just trying to make a living," I replied, bringing a bag of hot Cheetos to the register.

"One forty," he told me the cost, and I handed him a five-dollar bill.

"Add the rest to my account," I said, walking out the store. Instead of getting the singles and change back, I let him keep it, just in case, I was in a rush or if I didn't want to change out any money, I had a tab with them.

I trashed the small bag of chips before I even made it back to the car, a nigga was real muthafuckin' hungry plus I was running out of patience waiting on this nigga to slide through to get the yola.

"What's up?" I questioned the youngin' the moment he answered his jack.

"I'm almost there," he hollered over the music playing in the background.

I hated waiting on niggas especially when I was by myself. I had to move my eyes all around me. Out here in Lynchburg, I had to worry about the police and the hating pussy ass niggas that wanted to stick a nigga for everything that he had.

"Fuck that shit!" I slid behind the wheel, checking my rear-view mirror, making sure that I was good to move.

I pulled out from Z-Market and made a right. That nigga had to meet me over there by the Grey Hound bus station, fuck that shit with me waiting on him in the open. My freedom was a must and I wanted to keep it that way.

I pulled all the way down into the parking lot of the bus station by the train tracks and waited for dude to call me and come through, I was not taking this 6 duce back to the crib, fuck that. The second I parked my ride, my phone vibrated on my leg.

Yo bitch ass gonna learn, you can't keep puttin' ya hands on females, nigga. That shit is getting played the fuck out, for real. All you want to do is beat on bitches, but I bet you won't pull ya pants up and fight a real nigga.

I read the text message that the dumb bitch had sent me. With time on my hands, I replied.

And the next time, I see ya ass, I'ma make sure you swallow a few of them pretty white teeth that you have, on ya life, bitch. And when you find a real nigga that will square up with me, send him my way, bitch!

I hit the send button and leaned my seat back as Gucci played through the speakers as I watched my surroundings from every angle that I could, with the loud pack in my mouth.

Five Minutes later, my phone rang, "Murdoc, where you at, yo?" Byrd hit my line.

"Damn sure not in the spot you told me to meet you at," I snapped. Niggas had the game all the way fucked up.

"Mane, I got jammed up in some shit with my shorty, fam," he replied.

"That shit not my muthafuckin' problem, youngin'." The smoke exhaled from my mouth, slowly. "Come down to the bus station," I dropped the call, pulling the Dollar General trash bag from the console.

A few seconds passed before I saw the car moving towards my direction. This little nigga stayed flossing hard body, the ol' school Chevy could be spotted from a mile away. Orange and Blue paint job with 24 inches screamed *pull me over and search my car officer while I have this work on me.*

I shook my head as I watched him instruct the yellow bone female to park the car beside me with his hands.

The Chevy wasn't even parked fully, and the little nigga was jumping out the ride. Dress in a full Gucci outfit, with Gucci flip flops on his feet, I knew the little nigga was eating real fucking good.

He walked to the passenger side and leaned his head through the window, I had already placed the bag on the seat.

"My fault, yo," he reached his hand inside to dap me up. "Shorty was tripping about driving me." He dropped the money in my lap before our hands linked up.

"Nigga, you lucky that I waited on you, dawg. This the second time you did this shit, yo," I looked around, making sure shit was still Gucci.

"It won't happen again, homie. I'm for real, fam."

I nodded my head and put my hand on the wheel, as he picked the bag up from the seat, it was time for me to bounce.

I pulled off before he even got into his ride. The little nigga, Byrd, was hot as fuck, but his money was always correct so I couldn't even complain. But that shit had me questioning: was my freedom worth it fucking with his young nigga that loved to show the fuck off?

I made a right at the entrance and made the right at the light to hit Park Ave.

"Got Damn!" I hit the steering wheel as I watched the red and blue lights flashing behind me. "Fuck!"

Jamaica

Chapter 4

Love

I woke up with a headache from hell as I grabbed my belongings to hit the shower before I headed to my job-the compound beauty salon. My celly was long gone from the room, she was up at 5:30 a.m. faithfully every day, even on the weekends. As soon as the doors unlocked, she was a ghost. I respected how she respected my space and when I was asleep. The road was a two-way street. Doing time with a great bunkie was always a blessing and she was definitely a huge blessing. I cleaned my section of the room, getting it inspection ready before I bounced to the shower.

I picked my mp3 player up once I had cleaned up and hit the power button, I tapped the scroll button to get to my favorite artist, Jeezy. Once I got to his name, I pressed play, stuffing the buds in my ears and placing the mp3 player on my head as I wrapped my head up with my scarf, covering my ears carefully. I didn't want my earbuds to get messed up by a shortage or from the water.

Jizzle, by the Snow Man thumped in my ears as I exited my room.

Don't let me rip shit for ya
Still come through ya
Panoramic ass niggas
Yeah I shoot right straight for ya
Hole in ya nigga yeah you gon' need a ruler
The way I measure that, you can call me the ruler

It was 6:30 a.m., when I got to the shower, thanks to the clock that was posted up on the wall by the stairs that lead us up and down the tiers. No one was really up at this time, they usually woke up at 7, but not me. I had to get fresh every morning before I left the building. As I hit the curtain, I read the old lady's lips from Africa, *"Good morning, Love."*

I nodded my head and moved my mouth without uttering a word. *"Good morning."*

It was nothing better than hot water hitting your body in the morning, especially when it was ice cold outside. Down here in Alabama, it got cold and I wasn't a fan of the winter at all. I hated feeling cold and with that shit from Murda last night, I was still freezing.

Niggas were gonna hate me when I graced those streets again, on my life.

As Jeezy spat facts, I brushed my teeth and washed my body with a smile on my face. "I can't wait to be free!" I sang over the lyrics. My thoughts ran wildly thinking about all the shit I was going to do when they let me walk free.

Dead or alive, I was coming up out of this bitch, real.

***

Once I got dressed, I double checked to make sure the room was inspection ready, I damn sure didn't want the officer working today to stop by and do no damn search cause my room wasn't inspection ready.

"Morning, Love," Asia greeted me as I was walking down the stairs with my book bag hanging on my shoulder.

"Morning, boo," I replied, stopping to look at her hair all over her head.

"Can you fit me in today?" she smiled, seeing my eyes focused on her head.

"What are you tryna get done?" I was the only one that did her hair, once I started doing it.

"You know me, just freestyle it," she said, opening her room door, "you the beast at this hair shit, Love!"

"Already. I'll do it after count," I said, walking down the stairs, count was after 4 p.m.

I spoke to each person that spoke, as I walked to the computer to check my emails before I headed to work for the day. As I stood in line, I focused my eyes on the TV in the sports and newsroom not wanting to be looking on anyone. I was next in line.

As I entered my ID number and Pac number, I bopped my head to the music. I had seventeen new messages. Murda, Flowsicka, Qbanga, Snow and a few others had reached out. I hit Murda's message since it was the first one. He sent it at 1:30 a.m. 'cause it came through at 3:30 a.m. It took two hours for the messages to reach back and forth.

I fucked up, damn! I know this! Mane, I am so sorry that you are hurting because of my actions. I can't take it back, and if I could, I damn sure would. Fuck! I know you are not 'bout to call me back or even respond to this message. But I want you to know that it was never my intention to hurt you and the family that we were creating, on God. Shit happened, and now, I am here suffering, too. FUCK! Love, please just hear me out, that's all I am asking you.

I hit next 'cause it was from him too.

Bae, hear me out please, please!

I clicked the next message that was from Flowsicka.

Sissy, what's gud with you? It's Friday, the first, and you already know what time it is. Trappin' ain't never dead, these niggas just scared, all in my Jeezy's voice, LOL. But you know how shit is, but I *'ma hit you later. Hold ya head and I'ma stay screaming FREE YOU, till that shit is real! I love you*

I replied: *Sissy, what it do? And I already know if it's the first and it's on a Friday what time it is. Trappin' ain't never dead but snitchin' is real and niggas hate harder on a bitch than a nigga, so keep ya eyes wide open and stay on alert. HMU when you can and I love you, too! I can't wait for these muthafuckas to free a real bitch!*

I clicked on send, ready to read the next message which was from Snow.

Hey, girl, I know I have been missing for a while, but the love is still the same, I want you to remember that.

I hadn't heard from Snow for almost a year now. I knew how the free life was on the outside. Out of sight, out of mind. I couldn't blame anyone for anything, I had put myself in this situation and no matter what happened, even if I had to travel this road by myself, I was going to be okay and be a G about it. I had refused to let anything, or anyone bring me down. Fuck that shit and all the muthafuckas that counted me out.

I didn't even finish reading her email, I moved to the next and it was from QBanga.

Love, hit my line when you get this message, asap!

I didn't know what Murdoc's stepbrother wanted but since G was always 1 hunnid with me, I made a mental note to hit him up when I got off from work later.

Knowing my sperm donor, I was thinking that he had asked his brother to reach out to me. As I scanned over the other messages, I smiled seeing how others had missed a real one from the streets.

Love, I see you as the ultimate female, the true meaning of a strong black woman, far from the average. Your ability to love so deeply and risk everything including happiness and freedom for others happiness is unmatched. And your pain is so real, I feel it when I see pictures of you and hear your story. You once were a block of wood but over the years of being chiseled and carved by God's plan for you, you've become a beautiful masterpiece. Your downfall was being loyal and real and even though it took you away, it's what makes you so amazingly great. You are one person that deserves all the blessings in the world. Any man that gets the time of day with you, is the luckiest man alive. He will have the most beautiful, warm, loving go getta that God's ever created. You're an inspiration and a legend. It's not a lot but check ya account. Hold ya head, Queen.

I exited the message section, and tapped on my account, 600 dollars was deposited in my account. *"What a blessing,"* I said to myself. "Thank you, Lord," I said, clicking all the way out the Trulincs ready to hit the main door for work with Jeezy bumping through my speakers.

I would respond to the messages that needed a response later.

***

My day inside that beauty salon was long as fuck, I was happy as hell when the compound officer announced, "Yard recall!" I did about six hair dyes, plus wash and blow dry, and I braided two Studs hair.

"How was your day?" My home girl, Nique, asked me as I walked out the shop, she was coming from the library.

"Fucking long!" I had been knowing her for about two years now. And so far, our friendship was solid. I did her hair, also.

"You do the best, that's why you stay booked the fuck up." I frowned a little, but then we chopped it up as we walked towards our dorms. I lived in A1 and she lived in B2. "Are you going to dinner tonight?" She changed the subject because she knew I didn't want to talk or say shit else bout hair.

"What's for dinner?" I asked in front of my building as we stopped to watch the police officers talking in a group. Duncan, Belser, Williams and Polk were in a deep conversation as they pretended to be doing their jobs. These were the best officers that the compound had, they didn't give a fuck bout anything, so we made sure not to give them any problems. Making their jobs easy.

"Pork," Nique said, "but I know you are not feeling that shit," she started walking off cause it was yard recall, and we had to be inside the building before the yard was closed.

We had ten minutes to get everywhere we had to go and if we didn't comply, we were sent to the lieutenants' officer. And it all depended on the one in charge at that moment. Lt. St. John was cool but if she was pissed the fuck off, it was hell.

"Hell naw," I looked around, wondering when all this shit would be over for me. "I gotta do hair, plus I got something I can put together," I yelled to my friend as I stepped closer to the officers.

"Damn, I know ya job easy, but y'all ain't gotta make it look this easy," my face was twisted up into a smile as I spoke.

Belser, the shortest one of the crew spoke, "It's free, money!" And they all busted out laughing. This shit was getting mad old to me, and I was ready as fuck to get out of here!

Jamaica

"Fuck this shit" I yelled to the top of my lungs, fuck anyone that was around and heard me, I wish a bitch would say something. Today was not the day for real.

Chapter 5

QBanga

"Mane, you heard how that bitch played that nigga?" Phat spat to me as I twisted up the skunk. "That nigga been plotting on that nigga down fall for a minute," he continued dropping his head as I kept rolling the blunt.

I was ready to get my day started. And there was no other way than getting that good smoke to my lungs.

"What are you speaking on, G?" I pulled the lighter from my pocket.

"Oh, you ain't heard the news, Folk?" He questioned and I paused what I was doing to let him know I didn't by shaking my head.

"Mane, the nigga, Fool, sleeping with one of the G's lady."

"What?" I put fire to the blunt. "Who?"

"G, you are not ready for what I am about to spit at you."

I took a puff from the blunt, waiting on the news. Nothing with niggas surprised me these days, but to hear something from our Growth and Development Guys had me sitting the fuck up. Our bond between the brothers was to be unbreakable. Principles and morals were codes that we took seriously. The tattoo *Loyalty Out Values Everything* on my chest was what I stood on and I didn't expect anything less from anyone. What I gave out, I needed it all the way back in a stack and more. But I knew envy and pussy could fuck anything up that was good. But not with me.

"BankRoll," Phat said, dropping his head for the second time since we were vibing. "G," he continued, "Fam showed that nigga so much love that it's crazy. It has me looking at niggas in the crew mad different, yo."

I didn't reply, I took two extra puffs while hearing the news. "How y'all figured this shit out, fam?" I tried to pass the blunt to Phat, but he denied my love with me sharing.

"Mane, the nigga, Fool's, sister called BankRoll and told him." My nigga stared out into space with disappointment written all over his face. Fool must have pissed him the fuck off for her to turn on her own blood like that. *Damn!*

I knew he didn't expected shit like this to happen in the crew, but I knew when pussy was involved, niggas would tell on their own kids just to have the upper hand.

I had heard BankRoll telling Fool one night how he had to check up on some high bright chick from NC. I checked that nigga BankRoll, too, telling him he should never tell no nigga such thing, especially when he had a cookout at his crib almost every damn weekend.

"Niggas is always 'round ya wife, fam," we were like brothers, grew up with each other. Our fathers ran the streets together back in the 80's. "And you already know how niggas mouth be moving G."

"G, all the niggas in the circle is family, bruh," he spoke with his trust and head high.

I replayed the conversation to Phat, and the only thing he said was, "Damn!"

"When niggas let other niggas know their secrets, their deep secrets, nothing surprised me when it came to it been revealed, especially over some pussy, remember that, Fam." I preached to him. "But not all the niggas is like this, G. Realness separates a few niggas out the circle, and no matter how hard we try to trust everyone around us, especially the ones we call brother, it will always be a snake right under us."

"That means he had been checking his wife out the whole time," he spoke looking out on the road watching the kids playing on the basketball court across from my house. "I could never cross my brothers like that G, never!" He faced me and I saw pure sincerity in his face, and I felt his words. Realness stood out with my G in front of me.

"Yea, Fool had all intentions to tell BankRoll's old lady. And I bet that's how they ended up fucking with each other." I rapped to my dawg. "But Shorty should have been strong enough to put BankRoll up on the game that Fool was kicking to her, so it's both of them to be blamed."

"Loyalty is a big thing with me QBanga, I stand on it ten toes down," he said, walking away.

Yea, loyalty was always a nigga's favorite word, but his actions have to be able to back that shit up. Show me that *Death Before Dishonor* was not just a saying but it was a lifestyle that niggas took to the heart.

I hadn't spoken to BankRoll, but I knew deep down inside my nigga was hurting, that was his baby ma, his wife. The one that he gave his heart and soul to, the one that he tossed bricks at the penitentiary to give everything to. And to be mad honest, if that was my old lady, fuck her being my baby ma and wife, that bitch would be six feet under with fresh roses on top, courtesy of her pussy and being mad disloyal. I would raise my daughter without her ass, never telling her what the fuck really happened. *"Oh, ya mom had cancer."* Fuck that bitch and those ten years that we had been together.

"It's the same niggas in our faces that will damage us!" I yelled out as I put fire to the blunt.

I had four kids and four baby mothers, three boys and one girl. Shit was mad crazy but somehow, I was making it happen with working and hitting the streets on a regular, fucking with a few people that I knew were gravy. I had a shorty on my side that I've been fucking with going on seven years now. Yes, I had cheated on her twice, having two kids along the way, but somehow, she stayed grounded and stood by my side.

Sometimes, I wondered why and then other times, I figured it was the love that she had for me. But my heart and feelings were no longer there. I had my eyes on someone else. Someone that I knew was worth the wait and the journey that I had to travel just to get her. I knew I was going to catch hell just trying to get to her, but she was worth all the pain and trouble that I had to face. Sad thing is, I never even got a whiff off the pussy. "Got Damn!"

***

"Bruh, I have been trying to touch bases with you all day, G" BankRoll said to me the moment I answered his call, walking through the front door of my job. My day was over with and I couldn't wait to hit the gym. I was my routine, daily.

The conversation from early this morning with Phat was still fresh in mind, so when I heard BankRoll's voice on my line, I knew my family was about to pour his heart out to me.

"Yo, shit is fucked up, fam," he said, coughing and hearing his voice for the first time with this situation. I knew my nigga was fucked the hell up 'cause he never started our conversion ever with no shit like that.

"Speak to me, G." I walked to my car, watching my coworkers get into their vehicles, ready to get the fuck out the parking lot. This welding job was good, but damn, it was mad draining. It was times where I wanted to just dive headfirst into the game again, instead of just doing it on the side and say fuck this job.

"Mane, shorty fucking the G, Fool, fam!" The pain that I heard in my brother's voice touched my heart.

"What you wanna do 'bout the problem, bruh?' I asked opening the car door to my Audi. "All you have to do is say the word, fam." I meant just that shit. I knew if it was me, that nigga would be at my side plotting it all the way out.

"I gotta let muthafuckaz know shyt is not a game."

"Run the shit down to me, G."

"QBanaga, I am on my way to ya spot."

"Say less!" I said, dropping the call.

Chapter 6

Love

Once I got inside the unit, I made my way to the phone booth to place a call.

I dialed the number and said my name, removing my bookbag back from around my shoulder and turning down the volume on my mp3 player.

"What's up?" I said the moment they answered the call.

"Damn, is that how it is with us now?" He chuckled and I couldn't help but to smile, 'cause he was corny but yet, he was funny.

"QBanga, how are you doing?" I asked, leaning my back on the phone booth.

"Shit, I am good, the question is, how are you doing, G?"

"I'm good, ready for them to free me."

"Yea, I can't wait for them to do that." I heard a door closed, before he started talking again, "For real, I can't stop thinking about you."

I had to pull the phone away from my ear to make sure I was hearing what I was hearing from this nigga. "What?" I questioned, tapping my feet wondering what the fuck was really going on.

"I know this shit might sound crazy, and it finally hit me the other night when I saw your pictures on the book."

I was still in shock, so I didn't say a word. I just waited on him to continue.

"I know I am Murdoc's half-brother, but that shit is only by marriage, nothing more, Love. I know what you might be thinking, like this shit is crazy."

"Right!" And we both busted out in laughter.

"I can't change how I am feeling about you, I know you been through a lot, and for real, I have grown the fuck up, too, I am not that same little nigga that you used to look out for." He was all over the place, but I knew exactly what he was saying. "Just hear me out."

"I'm listening, QBanga."

"I know you got some time, and I am cool with riding the wave with you. Yes, I got some shit I got going on out here, but for real, it ain't what it really is," he paused and I could tell that he was jugging with some keys.

"What you think, ya stepbrother gonna say about all this shit that you spitting at me," I respected his words but damn, he was my sperm donor's step brother.

"What can that nigga really say? Huh? Nothing?" He asked the question and answered it himself, before continuing telling me how he was feeling. "When that nigga had you, he should have kept you. Niggas don't know how to love, treat, respect and be loyal to a real female. They rather have a bad bitch, than a real bitch."

"Right, but how do you know I am not taken?"

"Cause if you was, I know you. You wouldn't even entertain what I am saying to you right now, Love. I have been knowing you for a long time, and I pay attention to people, especially those that I care about, or want to know more about."

"Hit my Corrlinks, I got mad shit to do this evening," I said, laughing and not commenting on his remark.

"What all do you have to do?"

"Hit my Corrlinks, we'll rap about it." Instead of me hanging up, I had to ask him again about the little beef that him and Murdoc had back in the day. "But didn't Murdoc sleep with one of ya joints back in the day?"

I replayed the story in my head that me and QBanga had when I was free.

"So, I'm fucking with this bitch name Lotoya, but shawdy ain't my main joint, you feel me?" I nodded my head yes.

"Shawdy got a baby daddy that's locked up in the Feds so I was just knocking her walls down until her nigga, Cake, touch land. Anyway, two nights in a row, I've been calling the bitch, but she ain't been answering. The bitch lives out in Timberlake so I'm like what the fuck is up with her? Remind you, I've got a key to her crib, so I let myself in and guess who I see dicking her down?"

"Tamaine?"

"Yea, that nigga!"
Damn, that nigga can't keep his dick to himself. *"They didn't*
even hear me until I cocked the hammer on my .9."
"Yes," he answered my question. "But shorty can't be put in the
same sentence as you, it's a big difference. You are in a whole lane
by yourself, I'll kill for you, spend the rest of my life doing time
for you." His words took me back. "You are loyal, you don't depend
on anyone to take care of you and your kids. You are a natural born
hustler. At any cost, you are going to make sure of that. And you
bless people that are around you constantly. I am attracted to that."
"Boy, hit me later," I said, blushing from his words.
"Hold ya head, G."
"The only time, my head is down is when I am praying and
giving my nigga some head." I banged the phone on its base. I knew
my comment had him all the way fucked up. But it was the truth,
I'll never let muthafuckaz see me sweat.

***

Right after my phone call, I made a dash for it to the computer
to check my messages, the unit officer would be yelling *lock down*
in about fifteen minutes for the 4 p.m. count. I logged into my
account only to see fifteen messages in my inbox. So, I clicked on
them in order.

Murda: *Mane, I know you hurting, Love. But I am telling you*
that shit is not what you really think. I made a mistake, WTF. At
least talk to me, please. You 'bout to just give up on a nigga like
this!

Just seeing his pity ass emails in my fucking inbox made me
sick, everything about him, turned my stomach upside down. He
allowed my heart to turn cold due to his actions. Thank God, I was
locked up when he did this shit, cause only God knew what I would
have done, but since I was caged up and the only thing I had was
phone, mail and emails, I decided to hit him one last time with my
thoughts.

Murda,

You wanna keep talking 'bout me hurting, nigga when you do you ever know me to let what a nigga do to destroy my feelings? Never! You made ya mistake, so you learn from it, not me. Now you have to live with it. I don't have to talk to you, for what? So, you can keep repeating how sorry you are? Hell fucking no. Miss me with that shit. But let me say this, if you were locked up and I had got pregnant, how do you think it would affect your feelings and our relationship? Oh, let me guess, it's a different story, right? Oh, a nigga can do whatever, but let a female do it too, and she is labeled all kind of names. Niggas be so mad when females are on the same shyt they on. So, you should already know how I am coming. What's wrong, twin? Give up on you, shit ya dick gave up on US! I am not mad, far from it. But know this, Karma is a bitch, take it how you wanna take it. And if you feel like you want to take it in blood, I'll be free soon, you can come check me pussy! Fuck you, nigga!

I hit the send button, with a smile on my face cause what I was about to do next was about to kill him, slowly. I exited out of my inbox to enter my contacts, searching for his information, once I got to his name, I hit delete. He would receive my last message, but he would never be able to respond to my message unless I re-added him over and that damn sure wouldn't happen.

"Nigga, will see me on the land soon!" I said to myself checking the time on my watch, making sure I had enough time to check the rest of my messages. I was finished right on time with my messages, cause the officer started yelling.

"Lock down! To ya rooms, now!"

I hate when we have a female officer working the unit. Them bitches came in here on a power trip, daily. It's like this was the only place where they had control at. You could hear the whispering from the inmates: *Fuck that bitch! Look at her lace front.* And as I walked past her, I couldn't help but to let my eyes travel to her hair. It's funny how muthafuckas had the chance to leave here every day to go home but came in looking like they weren't free with the real supplies.

I made it to my room only to find my celly, Ms. Kanell sitting on her bed in her dark greys, reading the Bible.

"Hey, bunkie," I said, hanging my bookbag up on my clothing section.

As we waited for the count, we caught up on each other's day. With her working in the Chapel, she let me know what new movies were available. And I let her know that I made her appointment with hair stylist Kim.

"Thank you, Love."

"No problem, it's nothing to thank me for."

I redirected my attention to my stomach. I was hungry, I needed a snack cause I damn sure didn't have the time to make it to dinner. So, I unlocked my locker looking for the hot Cheetos to munch on.

"Have you heard about the new drug law, Love?"

"What new drug law, bunkie?" My appetite was gone, when it came to me fighting for my freedom, everything else was last, fuck the snack. I closed the locker back. Standing the hell up like a wall, I focused all my attention to her as I listened closely as she explained to me about the new drug law.

"So, all I have to do is file the motion for a time reduction under the two-point drug law?" I asked excited as fuck for the news.

"Yes, that's it. And there is a girl that works in the law library that lives in A2 and I can send her to talk to you at your job, if that's cool with you?"

"If it's cool with me? Shit, excuse my language, it's all the way cool with me." I was in a way better mood from this morning. All they could say was yes or no. I prayed for the best, but in the end, I knew firsthand how fucked up the system was. So, I expected the worst in the end.

Once the officers counted us and opened our doors, I hit the shower. I wanted to have enough time to do Asia's hair and use the phone before it was lock down time.

Doing Asia's hair was always great, we talked about everything that there was to talk about. But once she got on the topic of the new drug law, my heart started beating faster.

"They said that if you didn't get the two-point drug law when you were sentenced, you can get it now."

"Shit, I didn't get shit!"

"It's about time they start showing us drug dealers some love, Love."

I had all kinds of thoughts running through my head. Once I had called my kids, I was going up stairs to look over my paperwork from the courts.

An hour and half later, I was done doing the Starburst braids with the middle twisted into box sections.

"Girl, you did ya thing!" Asia said, checking her braids out in the mirror, sounding satisfied as ever.

"And you already know." I packed up my hair bag, washed my combs and my hands. As soon as Asia walked out the hair care room, I heard someone telling her, *"Your hair looks good, I know Love did that!"*

I got on the phone and spoke to my babies. Tameia was doing good, as usual, and Tamaine Jr. was giving trouble as always. "You have to be good for grandma and Mommy, okay?"

"Okay, Mom. I will."

"Good, I love you, let me talk back to Tameia." Once he gave baby girl back the phone, it beeped letting me know that I had a minute left. "I love you and I will call y'all tomorrow."

"We love you, too, Mom, and we can't wait until you are home with us."

The call dropped and my day lifted, thanks to my babies.

Chapter 7

Murdoc

As I pulled over in the church's parking lot, I had one thing on my mind, getting the fuck away. The second I put the car in park, I slung the door wide open and let my feet do the talking. I was not going to jail today and damn sure wasn't 'bout to give up all this bread that I just risked my freedom for.

"Stop running!"

I heard the officer yelling, but that bitch ass muthafucka had to either catch me or shoot me.

I heard the tires behind me and that made me move faster. The sound of sirens got louder, and it pumped me up. Fuck the police, today was not the day for me to go down, I hyped myself up and I dipped through the alley.

It was small enough for my body to travel, and that was a blessing, it gave me enough time to catch my breath, as the police car came to a halt. I looked behind and smiled knowing I had to get the fuck away from the area fast. I took off the black T shirt that I had on, rocking my white wife beater. A day like this, I wished I had Love around. Shorty would have been here picking a nigga up, without any questions asked.

As I made it through the alley, I stopped seeing that the police had given up, but I knew it wasn't for long. These Lynchburg officers got a hard on, locking us young black men up, daily. Today, it wouldn't be me.

"Murdoc!" I heard someone yelling at the top of their lungs from the left side of me on their porch. That bitch luck was on my side today.

"Who that?" I asked, moving towards their crib, thanking God for allowing me to get the hell away from those pussies.

"Cuzzo," he said.

The closer I got, I realized that it was my cousin, E.

"Fam, when you moved here?" I jumped up on his porch.

"A few months ago, yo." He paused, squatting and looking behind me, "I saw ya car on my way home surrounded by Tech and the dogs, fam." By the time he came up from crouching, I was already in his crib.

He closed the door, and I took off to the front window to peek out the blinds. I didn't see anyone with blue on and I was thankful for that. But I knew what was next, so I called Shorty.

I rang that bitch's line six times, and she didn't even answer. So I asked fam to use his phone, he walked away and came back with it. I dialed Shorty's number and she answered on the first ring.

"Wooooooo," I took a long breath of fresh air as I sat the fuck down holding my head in my hand. "Ayo, it's me," I said, trying my best not the fuck to go slap off on this dumb bitch. "I just got pulled over. And I need you to call the car in stolen, that way you can go pick it up, or else we are not going to get it back at all."

"Where did you get pulled over at, Tamaine?" She sounded pissed off, but I didn't care how she was feeling at the moment. She better be lucky it's just pissed off and not pissed on.

"Right over there by Miller Park." I rubbed my temples, closing my eyes, feeling the pressure of this shit on my plate, "The car in the church's parking lot."

"Coming from which way?"

"What the fuck? You not understanding what the fuck I am saying? Hello?" I looked at the phone only to see the wallpaper looking up at me. Instead of calling her back from E's phone, I used mine.

"Ayo, come on, mane." My tone was way calmer than it was seconds ago, I needed this bitch to handle this shit for me, but after this shit, it was damn sure a wrap for me and this bitch.

"It's the church right at the intersection. Can you go to Campbell Ave, or Park Ave or to go to E.C Glass, it's right there at the corner at the light?"

"Alright!" She hung the phone up in my ear.

"Mane, that hoe is gonna make me beat her ass, yo!" He came into the living room with a bottle of water for me.

"Fam, you gotta learn how to handle shit a different way, yo."
He handed me the water bottle as he continued his speech. "Women
are our Queens, fam. They need to feel love and know that the
protection will always be there, not being scared and hurt by the
hands that are supposed to cherish and honor them."

"Fam, sometimes, we have to treat some of them like that,
though," I said, pulling out a bill to hand to him. "Can you run me
up the street to see what's up with these pigs and then to the spot?"

"Yea, I can. But you don't need to pay me nothing for anything
I do for you. We are family, and as family, we have to have each
other's back." He told me as he picked his keys up off of the glass
table.

***

The area that I got pulled over at was surrounded by cops and
dogs. I pulled the fitted hat down over my forehead, allowing only
the bottom of my eyes to see anything. "Just drop me off at my spot
on Landview, fam."

"Bet!" He turned up the music as I replayed the whole situation
from me meeting that nigga, till the boys in blue got behind me. *Did
that nigga give me up? Or were the boys just doing their job?*

E pulled to my spot and I offered that bread again, and he
refused it the same way he did the first time.

"We family!"

I thanked him like twenty times before he pulled off.

I made my way inside of the crib safe, looking around to make
sure I didn't see anyone that was out to get me. This was my main
spot, so I wasn't really worried about anything to really happen
here. I was just being cautious. No one really knew this spot, plus I
didn't keep anything in here that would get me into something that
I couldn't get myself out of.

"What did they say when you called and reported the car
stolen?' I asked Shorty as soon as she picked up the phone.

"They ain't said shit really," her voice was as calm as the lake
at night.

"Nothing?"

"Naw, they just asked the regular and I told them the info."

"Alright that's a bet, let me know how much it's going to be to get it out the pound."

"Okay," she replied, hanging the phone up.

The moment she hung up, I got the call from Byrd, "What's' good, nigga?"

"I heard the boys pulled you over, so I am just checking to make sure you straight, yo." I knew the city talked fast so I didn't expect anything less. "Yea, I'm straight, but I'ma hit you later, yo." I ended the call, counting up the bread that I had on me all together.

The second the money hit the table, I heard the front door coming off the hinges.

"Lynchburg Police Department! Put ya hands up!"

Chapter 8

Love

I checked my email one more time for the night before I hit the sheets, and to my surprise, I had an email from QBagna.

Him: *I know our conversation from earlier probably had you off balance, but knowing you, I know you didn't even think about the conversation after we got off the phone, hahah. I can't deny how I am feeling about you, and you don't have to worry or stress about what people are going to think about you fucking with me. And that situation with your kids' sperm donor, that nigga is not related to me, but I am a man of morals and principles, so I have to bring it to his attention with how I am feeling about you. I am straight forward and I would rather a nigga come to me, man to man, and tell me what's up, than doing it behind my back, so let me handle that shit for you, fuck it, for us. I am telling you now, you fucking with a Boss, baby girl. I know what kind of niggas you had in ya life, and I am telling you now, I am not one of them, I am from a cloth that can't be cut or duplicated. My heart pumps real blood, I am stamped and certified to the core. I want you, fuck it. And when I want something, I go for it, and I am coming for you.*
Hit me Back.

I had to read that email twice and for real, I couldn't help the smile from appearing all over my face. As I hit the reply button, I turned my headphones up, jamming to Booise's song, *My Struggle*.

Once I was done, I got up feeling way better than I did, last night. Lost a nigga and gained fifty. One thing 'bout me, I never had to find a nigga, them thuggas found me.

I was on my way to my room when Shonda stopped me.

"Love," I pulled my headphones off my ears. "The counselor yelling your name," she said, pointing into Ms. Burkes direction.

"Thank you." I whispered, wondering what the hell she wanted with me this time of night. One thing about me, I didn't do the police. I didn't give a fuck if they were the Priest, once they worked here, they were the people to me.

"Yes," I greeted her once I was in her presence.

"I need to see you," she said, leading her way into her office that was outside the sports and news TV room.

"So, you put in a transfer for camp?" She took a seat in her chair behind her desk.

"Yes, I did!" The door closed behind me as I continued to stand.

"Well, your paperwork is making its way around the compound, once it gets to the Warden's desk, I will know something," she was clicking away at her computer, never making eye contact with me. One thing I hated the most was that. I gave people my full attention when I spoke to them, respect was due to a dog. But since I was an inmate, I guess I wasn't a human being, first.

"Thank you," I said, turning around to leave her office but her words made me stop moving.

"Do you know someone by the name of C. Wood?"

The name made my blood boil inside. Fifteen years of my life was taken away because this bitch ass nigga couldn't keep his mouth close. He told on me and the entire city, eighteen muthafuckin' people to be exact. He sold his soul to the people for his freedom rather than standing on principles and morals and the codes of the street life.

"Yes, I know who that is?" I turned to face her. She knew I knew him, it stated that we were codefendants in the paper work. "Why?" I asked, playing just as dumb as her.

"Because he is getting out in a year, and his paperwork is getting done. And since he is getting out first, plus he is going back to Lynchubrg, Va, you have to relocate to a different state."

Pussy ass nigga had a separate T, put on me, meaning that we could never be in the same state together by the government, this was their way of protecting him. He claimed that I had put a hit out on him and since he is protected by the police, they catered to him. Them mufuckas had the nerve to come at me about having his life in danger back when I was in the county jail. My mind traveled back to the day of the visit that I got.

"Ms. Jenkins," Ms. Randoo, the chocolate quiet officer woke me up from my bed, "You have some visitors waiting on you."

"Where is Ms. Allen?" I asked, putting on my jumper. I was still in the county jail in Lynchburg. Ms. Allen was mad cool and I was used to her as an officer, but Ms. Randoo seemed down to earth as well. "She is in H pod today." She said, opening up the room door with calling control.

"You know who is here to see me?" I questioned her as we walked to the main door.

"No, not really. But they do look like some real big people." Her answer gave me a hint.

"It ain't gonna be long, if I think who I think it is, so stay around!"

Once I got to the booth, I didn't even take a seat, I paced the small section back and forth as I waited to see who the fuck wanted to see me.

Minutes passed before anyone came, just as I was about to hit the glass section of the door and tell Ms. Randoo to get me the fuck outta there. I heard voices behind me.

I turned around to see two white muthafuckas staring at me with smirks all over their faces.

"Ms. Jenkins, take a seat." The taller one said, but I rolled my eyes, that made the other one mad. His face turned red as a tomato.

"You might need to take a seat, young lady!"

"This my house, fuck I look like taking orders from you?" I was already locked up and I knew the time I was going to get was going to be long, so I made myself comfortable. Fuck these muthafuckas that were trying to break me. "Talk and talk fast, cause I ain't got time!" I chuckled, no one will ever break me and see it.

"You will be served with another indictment," the tall cock sucker said with a smile wide on his face.

"Serve that bitch, then!" I said, gritting my teeth. One thing 'bout me, I refused to break, fold or fumble under any pressure.

"Two more years will be added to your time for having a confidential informant's life in danger!"

"Fuck you! Fuck him!" I pointed at the short one, "And fuck that pussy nigga that snitched on me! And y'all can't charge me with shit, y'all don't have me on the phone, no mail, not a muthafuckin' thing!" I screamed at the glass. "Take them charges and shove them up y'all asses!" I turned around and banged on the door, never looking back at the pussies behind me.

"Yes, I know that we can't be in the same state as each other," I said, smiling away at my counselor. "I'll figure this shit out, I still have time to do." I turned and walked out of her office. The entire fifteen minutes that I was in the office made me sick just listening to her.

"Get me the fuck outta here!" I yelled to the top of my lungs, causing everyone to look in my direction.

The entire unit got silent. That bitch ass nigga was fucking up my whole fucking life.

My kids were still in the Burg, how the fuck was I going to explain to them, that I couldn't come back to where they were. I felt the tears swelling up in my eyes, but allowing them to fall would never happen.

"Bitch ass nigga!" I yelled on my way to my room.

Chapter 9

Murda

Love's message fucked me up, especially when I recognized that I couldn't email her back. I knew her mouth was fya, but to be at the top of the flame, I was damn sure feeling the heat. My actions had caused me to fuck up something great. Kandi was three months pregnant and she was keeping it. I never asked her to have an abortion, even though it crossed my mind, but I couldn't. Shit was falling apart for me.

I leaned my head back on the sofa as I allowed the papa smurf weed to affect my body as I prayed silently hoping that the baby Kandi was carrying wasn't mine.

"Fuck!"

I needed to get in touch with my brother, Maurice, so he could get Flowsicka to hit Love up for me. They talked on a regular, so that was a blessing, at least I could log into her account and send Love a message telling her to fucking unblock me.

The more and more I ran bro's line, and he didn't answer, I started to expect the worse. The high that I was about to reach had gone out the window. So, I decided to shoot him a text, *Bruh, hit me ASAP!*

I had Flowsicka's number, but I never used it unless it was an emergency. I always vibed with Shorty through my brother, and since he wasn't picking up, I hit her line. When my call got sent straight to her voicemail, I knew something was up. The feeling that I started to feel in my gut was painful.

I jumped up off the sofa, grabbing my car keys and dropping the blunt in the ashtray. I dialed Maurice's phone number again, and this time, it went straight to his voicemail. That shit threw me way off balance.

"Fuck!" I stepped to the door, I had to find out what the fuck was going on with my family.

As soon as I got in my ride, I hit A-Town's line, fam answered on the first ring on my end. "Yo, what's good with you, nigga?" I spat, starting the engine up.

"Mane, shit is fucked up!" The tone and words he used let me know shit was out of hand.

"Where you at?" I asked, pulling out the parking lot.

"I'm over here at Snow's crib?"

"Snow?" I asked shocked as fuck, the only Snow I knew was Love's best friend.

"Yea!".

I hadn't talked to ol' girl in a hot minute, so I didn't know if she was still in the same spot or she had moved, last thing I knew, she was still with the nigga Pedee. So, hearing bruh mentioning her name, really had me dazed the fuck out.

Why the fuck was he with Shorty? But that was not my business, my main business right now, was getting in touch with my brother.

"Have you talked to my brother?"

"Fam, him and Flow got jammed up last night," he said with pain in his voice.

"What?" I drove past McDonalds on Memorial Ave, seeing that the fuck boys had pulled someone over. They had the person sitting in the back of their car, as they tore the Chevy Impala apart. Two police dogs stood firm at their master's side.

"What time all this took place, bruh?" The light changed and I rode pass shaking my head.

"Shit late, fam, I am not trying to speak over this joint."

"What's the address?" I asked feeling defeated and wondering what the fuck really happened to my bruh and his girl.

"I'm out here in Timberlake, fam. Hit me when you get to Fridays and I'll direct you to me."

Nothing else needed to be said, I dropped the call and bust a U turn right at the intersection at E.C. Glass school. Fuck the police.

***

I hadn't heard from Smoke, so I hit his line. "What's good with you, yo?" I asked my nigga from the struggle. Our Bond was born through the struggle of this shit we called life. I trusted this nigga with everything, time and time had proven his loyalty to me and those that we had in the circle.

"Mane, I have been waiting on you to reach out to me." I heard the clippers in the background, letting me know that he was at the Barber shop. "You heard that shit, yo?"

"Yea," I answered, knowing he was referring to my brother and girlfriend getting jammed up. "I'm on my way out here to talk to A-town."

"Oh, yeah, I gotta speak with you on that situation, too." I heard him but seeing the fuck boys behind me made me drop the phone in my lap.

"Smoke," I yelled, "12 behind me, and the line in my lap." I signaled left, turning right at the plaza as they kept going, and then it hit me, the dick rider was on the way to the problem at McDonalds. I picked the phone up, pulling my .45 from my waist and sitting it on my lap, fuck going back to jail or getting hit up by the boyz. I am willing to ride for whatever. "Mane, I am back."

"Mane, you want me to make that move with you?"

"Naw, hold the spot down, I'll be back later to vibe with you, homie."

"Already!"

Fifteen minutes later and I was passing Fridays. I hit A-Town up and listened closely as he gave me directions to where he was located. By the time I pulled up in the driveway, five minutes later, my nigga was sitting outside with smoke coming from his mouth.

"What's good, nigga?" We dapped each other up.

"Bruh, that shit is crazy," he said, walking in front of me towards the front door.

Shorty's spot was out here in the cut, and I knew she was home 'cause her car was parked behind bruh's Infinity. She had switched up her spot, but her ride stayed the same. That nigga Pedee kept ol' girl fresh and decked out, but I kept wondering how the fuck did she and Town linked up.

"I'ma be in the basement, Snow!" He yelled as soon as we entered the crib. Her spot was laid the fuck out, portraits of Biggie and Jay Z graced the walls, the all-white wrapped around living room set shined with gold pillows. A huge 82-inch flat screen hung from the ceiling with the highlights of last night's game on. A small bar was sectioned off in the corner with all kinds of liquors on top of the counter. The scent of fresh vanilla filled the room along with some bleach.

The basement looked like a miniature apartment. The place was spanking clean. My nigga took a seat and dropped his head in his hands.

"Talk to me yo," I looked around the room, noticing a basket with a white tee, with sprinkles of blood on it. "A-Town, what's good, yo?" I walked over touching my nigga's shoulder. He pulled his phone out and showed me the unthinkable.

LYNCHBURG, Va. (WSET) - *Two people are behind bars, Wednesday night, after State Police say they found drugs on them. State Police say Maurice and Flowicka were arrested and charged with felony drug distribution offenses after intercepting a 250-pound package of marijuana at the post office.*

The drugs are worth a lot of millions. State police are still investigating.

"What the fuck?" I read the news over and over again. Taking a seat beside my nigga on the sofa, my head dropped, but I knew deep down that my brother was rock steady, and Flow's loyalty was just as strong, so I knew they were good. But damn! I told that nigga to chill, but no, the bread was coming in so fast that he wanted to keep going.

"Shit crazy, right?" Bruh said, breaking the silence in the room.

"Hell yeah!"

"Oh, that shit ain't shit, fam," he stood to his feet and walked to the bottom of the stairs, staring upstairs. "I hit a nigga all the way up last night," he said, walking back towards me. I glanced over at the clothes and he shook his head. "Yea, that way! Pussy nigga thought he could just take the stand and point a nigga out and nothing happen!"

Niggas forgot that loyalty was a must, but real street niggas handled pussies even if the problem didn't have anything to do with them. Real niggas stood on codes of the streets, respect, trust, and loyalty.

"Principles and morals fam," he said, throwing me a bag of weed and a dutch. "I will never associate myself with niggas that snitch, take the stand, none of that shit, and if I run across a nigga that did something like that, especially to my nigga or someone that I fucks with hard body," he pulled the hammer from his waist, "I'ma chalk that muthafucka, dawg."

"What the fuck happened, bruh?" I asked as I rolled the blunt up for us to blaze.

"I'm coming out of the club, right? So, I see this nigga Tony S, right?" he said, pacing the room back and forth. "That's the nigga that took the stand on Mr. RunitUP, bruh."

"Yea, that's that nigga's name," I licked the blunt, "yea, that's the bitch ass nigga name, Tony S."

"I already couldn't stand the nigga, 'cause he stayed throwing salt on nigga's names in the streets, but when I saw the paperwork from Mr. RunitUP, it was a wrap for me. I told Shorty go to the car, I'll meet you there. So, she left, and I followed this nigga all the way out the club."

"Word?" I added fire to the blunt. Bruh was built for this shit all the way around. He lived what niggas rapped about.

"Mane, you know me. As soon as the nigga's foot touched the concrete and wasn't inside the club no more, fam, I leaned all the way back and rocked his ass."

I busted out laughing 'cause I could see that shit now playing out. "Bitch ass nigga. My fist connected with his jaw, and I swung again, but I missed and the nigga caught my chin. I staggered back but came back with a two-piece combo. Nigga tried to pull out on me, fam, but I was way faster!" He pointed to the joint on the ground, showing me how he stood over that muthafucka and sprayed his ass with lead.

"Fam!" I stood up, knowing the whole fucking place was packed with cameras and eyewitness.

"I already know what you bout to say, yo." He took the blunt from my hand, "but if all niggas that screamed *loyalty* was like me," he tapped his chest, "the world would be a better place!" He took a puff of the blunt, "anywhere I spot a disloyal nigga, I'ma make him pay. Straight the fuck up!"

Chapter 10

Love

The lady that my celly had told me about, came to see me at the beauty salon.

"Can you meet me here at lunch time? If that's cool with you, and if it's not, just let me know when and where I can meet you?"

"Yes, Love. Lunch time is perfect for me. I'll see you at 11:30." She left me with a smile on my face. It was time to fight for my freedom, fucking fifteen years was a lot of time and if I could hand some of this shit back, I was willing to do just that.

I went back to work with hope on my mind. I did four heads from 8 until it was lunch time. As I waited on Joan to arrive, I felt peace all over me.

"Are you going to lunch?" Miss Kim asked, walking to the front door.

"No, I am waiting on someone to come see me." Nothing in prison was private, but I tried to make my life as private as I could. She didn't respond and I was cool with that.

When Joan showed up, I had all my paperwork for her that she might need to get the process going. "What are you going to charge me?" Nothing in prison was for free.

"Nothing," she replied, looking over the stack that I gave her.

"Nothing?" I asked studying her face, but it didn't change.

"It's my way of giving back to people here, Love." she smiled.

"Come on, mane, I can't let you do that for free."

"I want everyone free from this place of bondage. I'll let you know what I think by yard recall." And she was gone.

The time at work flew by and when it was time to leave, I was already ready to get the hell up out of there. Joan was at my building waiting on me with a brown envelope in her hand.

"You didn't snitch?"

"Fuck now! That shit ain't in my blood," I responded.

"Loyalty pays off," she handed me the envelope, "read over the paperwork on top, if it's of your approval, sign it and put it in the mailbox tonight."

"Compound close!" The officer yelled over the intercom causing us to cut our conversation short.

"Thank you!"

"No problem."

I didn't even check my emails, fuck that shit, I went straight to my room and got my clothes for the shower.

***

Once the count was cleared, I got on my bunk and got to work with the motion that Joan had filed.

In The United States District Court
For The Western District Of Virginia
Roanoke District
Case No: DVAW612cr00017-003/FVAW

<u>Love Jenkins,</u>
      PETITIONER
VS.

<u>UNITED STATES OF AMERICA,</u>
_____RESPONDENT
MOTION FOR REDUCTION OF SENTENCE PURSUANT TO 18 U.S.C &3582(C)(2) IN LIGHT OF RETROACTIVE EFFECT OF AMENDMENT 782

On July 18, 2014, the United States Sentencing Commission, unanimously agreed to the retroactive application of Amendment 782, subject to a special instruction. Amendment 782 generally revised the Drug Quantity Table and chemical quantity tables across drug and chemical types.

The proposed Amendment also provides a new application note clarifying that this special instruction does not preclude the Court from conducting sentence reduction proceedings and entering Orders, before November 1, 2015, provided that any Order reducing the defendant's term of imprisonment has an effective date of November 1, 2015, or later.

As I read all the information above, my head throbbed. And my heart raced, as I imagined that I would be able to regain my freedom.

In light of the aforementioned synopsis, the petitioner, Ms. Jenkins, proceeding pro se, humbly, comes before this Court, nunc pro tunc, requesting retroactive application of Amendment (782), as she qualifies under 1B1.10. In support thereof she states:

Ms. Love Jenkins was sentenced to a term of 180 months, followed by 5 years of Supervised release. Petitioner was convicted of violating Federal Statue(s) 21 USC 846 & 21 USC 841(b)(1)(a).

Everything that she had documented was great, it was excellent. She had gone and did her research and listed all the codes that were needed to help fight the case. Applying all the adjustments that needed to make it look good.

The court also considered public safety considerations. The petitioner does not pose a threat to society, as her crime was that of a nonviolent nature. The petitioner had attached her incarceration record, which is inclusive of her achievements, which are factors that will prevent recidivism. The petitioner has continuously worked on bettering herself to become an integral part of society, and not a burden to it.

As I read it, I smiled cause knowing those that were going to be reading this would probably be like, *She was a danger to the streets, she destroyed peoples' lives.* But it was all worth a try. A lot had changed, since I had been locked up. The streets made me but losing my freedom and not being there for my kids, killed me more than anything that there was to endure.

I signed and dated the paperwork, added the stamps on the envelope.

My celly had been gone all evening, so when she entered the room with a smile, I had to ask her what was up.

"I see Joan took the time to come see you," she said, getting her clothes ready for tomorrow.

"If it wasn't for you," I got off my bunk, "I don't know if I would have heard about this news," I said, hugging her.

"Love," she wrapped her arms around me, "you have been nothing but a blessing to my life, I want nothing but the best for you!" And I felt it, not just with her words, but her actions spoke well.

The moment I got out the door, the officer was yelling, *lock down*! Time had flown by so quickly that I didn't even get the chance to check my email or fix me something to eat.

"I gotta put this joint in the mailbox," I yelled to Duncan, ignoring his command that we lock down.

"Love," he screamed across the room as he locked room 101. "Really?"

"I gotta put this joint in the mailbox." I showed the envelope, smiling and throwing my hips just a little. Even though these niggas in here had bitches at home, they stayed flirting, so tonight I was going to be using their trick.

A nigga can do, why can't a bitch do it, too? Inmate or not. Pussy is pussy!

Chapter 11

Murdoc

"Lay on the ground! Hands above your head!" They yelled. My heart raced as I complied. "You have the right to remain silent, anything you say might be used against you in court of law."

"Y'all have a warrant?" One pig had their boot on my neck as one placed the cuffs on my hands behind my back. "What the fuck am I under arrest for?" I asked but no one answered or said a word to me.

They started tearing my crib apart, and as I watched I was happy as hell that I didn't have anything in the spot at all. They lifted me to my feet and ran my pockets.

"How much is this?" One officer asked, pulling the rubber band of money out of my pocket.

"Shit you can count, so count it! But tell me what the fuck am I under arrest for?"

"Where is the weapon that was used in the robbery?" The question caught me off guard that I almost stumbled into the wall still in the officer's possession.

"What?" I stared at the white man.

"Are you deaf or you didn't hear me?"

"Fuck you!" I spat at him. I would never tell on myself. But only one person knew about that robbery that took place.

Damn! I hung my head, feeling the hate and the betrayal.

***

I was booked into Blue Ridge Regional jail on multiple chargers that I knew all the way to well.

LYNCHBURG (WSLS) – *Police are searching for a man after he allegedly shot a man and stole his wallet. Lynchburg police currently have a warrant for 28-year-old Tamaine Davidson of Lynchburg. Police say the incident happened Sunday around 4 p.m...*

Only one person knew the facts about this situation. The driving with no license and eluding the police, was nothing, but that shooting shit was serious, especially if the nigga showed up to court and pointed me out.

"Gotdamn!" I kicked the steel toilet. "Can I make a phone call?" I asked the officer from my intake cell. I was denied bond from the gate. My record was horrible. I had domestic charges, drug charges from both Lynchburg and Amherst county. This time I knew they were going to sit my ass all the way down. "Yo, can I make my one-time free phone call?" I shouted, but I got ignored.

My mom had my back at all times, but last time she told me that she was done with helping me get my shit together, especially when she was already raising my two kids that Love had with me. But I knew all that shit she said, she would never turn her back on me.

Chapter 12

Qbanga

The moment, I turned the knob to the front door, I heard, "You are fucking disrespectful," Shorty was screaming and approaching me with her fist balled up. "You fucking bitches left and right, and think I am just supposed to sit here and let you play me like a fucking game!" She was all the way up in my face. "It's okay for you to fuck but as soon as I do it, oh, it's fucking over, huh?" She pointed her finger in my face and I hated that shit more than anything in the world. "But you know what, you are not the one to be blamed for this shit!" She mushed my face with her palm, and everything in me wanted to smack the fuck out of her. But my days of putting my hands on females were long gone. If it was back in my younger days, I would have blacked both of her fucking eyes, and knocked her fucking tooth straight from the root.

"The fuck you tripping for, yo?" I moved her out my way.

"Why the fuck am I tripping? You think it's cool for you to go out here and get bitches pregnant and think it's okay for me to stay with your ass?" she chuckled behind my back. "QBanga, I am telling you, now," I turned around to face her.

"Tell me what you have to tell me, Kiara!" I stepped all up in her space. "Bitch, I am here taking care of you, spoiling you," I waved around the room, reminding her of all the things that I had done for her ass. "Name brands? You rockin' them. Look at your jewelry, you stay shining. Oh and let's not forget about you cheating on me!" Her face dropped. I know I said I would never bring it up, but when I thought about all the shit that I had done for her and then she stepped out on me, there was no way I would stop fucking bitches, until I found that one. "You was driving the nigga around in the whip that I busted my ass off for you." I was heated.

"But you cheated, you had two babies on me." She screamed.

"And you lucky as fuck I didn't body ya muthafuckin' ass!" I walked the fuck off on her. Fuck all that shit she was spitting.

Catching her ass cheating should have been the last straw, but I stayed with her.

I had just come home from doing seven years when I ran into shorty. A first everything was peaches and cream, but two years into our relationship, she started acting funny. She stopped coming home early, kept telling me she was visiting her family out of state every weekend. I trusted her, so I took her words to the heart not questioning her actions, until I caught her ass first hand.

"Where you said, you put the shoe boxes at, Kiara?" I was at the top of the stairs, as she stood at the bottom.

"They are in my closet to the back."

I made my way to her closet, finding it exactly where she told me it was, then I heard something vibrating.

"What the fuck?"

I stopped moving, trying to locate the vibration. I moved each piece of garment to the side until I found one of her purses in between her clothes on a hanger.

The second I grabbed the purse, the vibration started again. I opened the bag just to see a cell phone looking up at me with Bae flashing across the screen. A three pack of magnum condoms was also present. I answered the phone not saying anything,

"Baby," the nigga voiced, and I walked down stairs.

When Kiara saw me descending down the stairs with the purse and phone in my hand, her whole body stopped moving. I tossed the phone to her and she didn't even attempt to catch it, it fell at her feet.

"Go ahead, that nigga on the line, shorty."

I took a seat on the steps, watching her body shaking in front of me. I took the condoms out and tossed them at her. Her secret was out in the open.

"You done fucked up!" I said, picking my feelings up when I stood to my feet. "Do you, shorty!" And from that day our relationship changed.

I took a shower and hit BankRoll's line, "Fam, you on the way to see me?"

"I'm 'bout to pull up on you in like six minutes, G."

"Alright that's love, G, but I need you to meet me at the park," I said, putting my sneakers on. "Shorty tripping and I am not with that shit tonight, fam."

"Say less!" He dropped the call.

"You stay tripping on me leaving the crib, but you can do whatever you want though, right?" Shorty was heated, but I didn't give a fuck about her emotions. My nigga needed me and I was on my way to him, it always bro's before hoes, especially a disloyal one at that.

"Fuck that shit you spitting, slim!" I moved around her, "I don't have time for no bitch, so if it's that what you worried bout, then you shouldn't be," I gazed her down. "A bitch is the last thing that I'm worried about." I walked right out the door, never looking back.

Twenty minutes later, I was pulling into the parking lot of the Red Lobster. The moment I saw my nigga, I knew fam was hurting. It was written all over his face. "G," I embraced him, "how you holding up?" I released him.

"You already know, fam." He brushed his shoulders off. "That nigga has got to pay!"

"What about Shorty?"

"Fuck her! I'll deal with her later."

"Say less!"

Jamaica

Chapter 13

Murda

"What the fuck, yo!" I knew shit was definitely all the way real. Maurice was caged up, Flow was trapped, too, and now A-Town was damn sure on the run. "I gotta get everybody a lawyer, yo!"

I rubbed my head. The game was damn sure screaming my name harder than it was ever before. Slinging weed was not going to make it to support everybody. I had to come up with a master plan to hold shit down.

"How the fuck did you link up with Snow, though?" I switched up the conversation all the while thinking about linking back up with my plug.

"Shorty had been coming through the hood recently," he said, whispering and staring upstairs. "I knew who she was from Love, but we never really spoke, until she asked if I had seen Pedee."

"What's good with them anyway?"

"Bruh, it's so much shit, but I'ma give you the short version," he said, lighting the blunt back up and taking a seat.

Snow found out that Pedee was cheating on her all these years. Homie even had a 2-year-old baby boy named after him, too. She tried to make it work, but the nigga wanted to be where his kid were and since she didn't want to have any babies, she decided, if that's where he wants to be, there was no need to be holding him captive, so she let him go and moved on.

"What the fuck?" I never thought that their relationship would end the way it did. I guess the picture they painted wasn't all that solid.

"Yea," he puffed and handed over the blunt to me. "Shit's real, anyway. We started kicking it and shit and this is where it's at right now, fam." He looked off into space and I could tell that his mind was running mad hard.

It wasn't until his phone rang that either one of us spoke. "What?" He stood to his feet with his head down. "Hell no!" He started walking the room again. "What the fuck!" I could hear someone talking on the other end but I couldn't put together exactly what they were saying. "Mane, let me know what the fuck is up my nigga!" He hung the call up staring me down. "That nigga is alive, bruh!"

"What?" This shit was getting worse and worse by the second.

"I hit the nigga up like seven times!" He stood back against the wall, with disappointment written all over his face. "Bruh, I was standing over that nigga, yo."

"Muthafucka gonna identify you if someone else don't, my nigga!" I spat facts at him.

"I already know how the muthafuckas in this city is."

Lynchburg was full of fake muthafuckas and snitches, money out lasted morals and principles. And if a nigga thought you was on a path better than him and his, he was determined to take you out, even if he had to get the boys involved.

"But you know what type of nigga I am." I reached for the blunt that was almost done. "I'm never just going out like a succa, fam, muthafuckas better come correct."

***

As soon as I left A-Town, I called my big nigga in New York. "What's up, son? How are you?"

"Shit, my nigga, you already know what's jumping."

"Say less, I'ma make a trip up there to see you soon, son."

"Already, my nigga."

I wanted to speak to my brother to find out exactly what the fuck was going on with him and Flow. It had been two days and still no word from them. It was a must for me to find out what was going on. And no matter what was going on, I was going to be there for my family, my niggas. No price or bread amount could stop or hinder my love and loyalty for them.

The moment I pulled up at the barber shop, my phone rang. It was a number I didn't recognize.

"Hello," I answered, getting out of the car.

"Hey, your brother on the phone," an unknown female's voice spoke, "I'ma click over so you can talk to him."

"Bro," Maurice said. Hearing his voice, relaxed me.

"What the fuck, mane?" I got right to the point.

"Yea, shit crazy, yo. I need you to get me and shorty a lawyer, ASAP. They denied us bond," and I could tell a million thoughts were running through his head, 'cause he had yet to stop talking. "And Shorty gonna link you once I get off the phone with some information that I need you to handle, ASAP."

"Alright," I said, once he gave me the room to speak.

"Make sure you handle everything, bruh, and get someone to throw some money on our books, too."

"I got you. I'ma go holler at the lawyer. I was just waiting to hear from you."

"Yea, do that. And what's good with Town?"

"Shit, it's a lot, but when is ya visitation?"

"I think on Friday."

"Bet! I'll handle what needs to be done and you will see me on Friday," I said leaning on my ride.

"Love bruh," he spoke.

"Death before Dishonor, my nigga!"

Smoke was in the window, watching me, but as soon as he saw me put the phone in my pocket, the door flew open.

"I just got off the phone with Bruh, dawg."

As I updated my homie on what was going on with everything, he just listened, never interrupting me as I spoke. "I gotta make mad moves. I need you to have my back. Ya shorty gotta run the shop for us, until we are a few steps ahead of the game, bruh."

"It ain't nothing she can't handle."

My phone rang and it was the number that had called me with my brother on the phone.

"Hello," I answered.

"All right, this is what he told me to tell you," she started off and I just listened.

Chapter 14

Love
A Month Later

A lot had been going on in the land of the free. I heard that Flowsicka and Maurice had got jammed up. A-Town was on the run for aggravated, malicious wounding. My kids' father was also caged up according to Ms. Julia.

"Love, he is never going to change or try to better his life," his mom announced. "All he wants to do is what he is doing. He doesn't do anything for your kids, and when he does, it's nothing major. He constantly lying to them, promising them how he is going to do better and stay out of prison."

That nigga was the luckiest nigga ever fucking with the system. He stayed catching a break from the judges. Since I had been gone, he had been locked up like eight times, so far.

"I wish him the best," I uttered, meaning every word that I said.

"But this time, it looks crazy for him. I heard he even got a hostage charge."

"What? On who?" I asked, waiting to know.

"On some girl that tried to leave him."

"What happened to his other baby ma?"

"Girl, they got married, had a baby, but that didn't change him, he is still running around on that girl. Word on the streets," I cut her off with my laughter.

"Word on the streets though, Ma?"

"Yes, boo, word on the streets, she divorced him because he wouldn't stop beating and cheating on her."

"Damn!" I remarked not giving a fuck, that nigga will always be a woman beating, nothing surprised me with him. "I wish them the best."

"Mail call!" The officer yelled and the day room got mad loud.

"The kids good?" I questioned.

"Yes, girl. Tamaine is playing the game and Tameia is doing her homework."

"Well, I am not going to hold you. I love y'all and I'll call sometime this weekend."

"We love you, too, Love." I hung the phone up as I waited to see if I had any mail.

It was hard for me talking to my kids, I knew I hadn't been there but I tried my best to play a huge part in their lives, from calling, to buying things and writing letters. I made sure I stayed connected.

"Jenkins!" The office yelled.

I stepped through the crowd, whispering excuse me trying to make my way to the podium to get my mail.

"Jenkins!" He yelled again, as soon as I got to the front.

"Jenkins, right here," I held my ID up showing my card.

He handed me two pieces, and as soon as I turned to walk away, he called my name again, this time our eyes locked and he smiled.

"Jenkins!" I said my name, holding my hand out for him to put it in there.

"Is it your birthday?"

"Is that your job to know?" Everyone around me stopped talking. "Can I have my mail, please?" I bit my bottom lip, "Please?"

His eyes bucked and I smiled on the inside. Nigga don't try me just 'cause I am inmate. I was trained to go but fucking with the police was and never would be my thing.

I lingered around, waiting to see if I had any more mail. And once I realized that there wasn't any more, I walked in the direction of my room.

"Jenkins!" The officer yelled. I turned around, and watched him wave his hand in the air towards the office. I rolled my eyes and took a deep breath.

"What?" I asked when I walked into the office.

"Where are you from?"

"Why does it matter where I am from, you know where I am, right?"

When he didn't respond, I took my ass out of his office. "What did he want you for?" Shemika asked me.

"Shit!" I kept walking, and even if it was something, I damn sure wouldn't repeat what was said.

I couldn't wait to get to my room, I had a letter from the courts. My celly was gone when I opened the door and then I remembered that she was going to a prayer meeting with her best friend, Sam.

A letter from my kids' father, cause his dumb ass wrote his name on the envelope, one from the courts and one from an address that I didn't know.

Before I ripped open the one from the courts, I said a small prayer. "Lord, let this be good news."

United States District Court
For the
Western District of Virginia

United States of America
V.
Love Jenkins

Order Regarding Motion for Sentence Reduction Pursuant to 18 U.S.C 3582(c)(2)

Upon motion of (**X**) the defendant ( ) the Director of the Bureau of Prisons ( ) the court under 18 U.S.C 3582(c)(2) for a reduction in the term of imprisonment imposed based on the guideline sentencing range that has...

I skipped to the point. THIS MOTION is DENIED.

I tossed the letter on my bed, feeling the tears whelping up, but I pulled them back. I had put in too much hope and now I didn't know how to see the words, DENIED.

I took a deep breath and smiled, ripping the letter open from my kids' father.

Love,

What's good with you, nigga? I hope you are doing good; I know it's been a minute, but I know you already heard the news. Niggas hate me that much so I know there were happy as fuck to let you know that I was locked the fuck up, again. You stay throwing salt on my name, like what the fuck yo! I mean, you hate me that much that you don't want me to win. That's fucked up. I have been nothing but good to you. I try to be there for the kids, but my mom stay screaming how I can't see or get them. What the fuck!!! Muthafuckas don't fuck with me unless it's 'bout money. QBanga called himself trying to stunt on me, but fuck that nigga, we ain't blood, so you already know he don't mean shit. We just family through marriage, fuck that shit, we ain't even family. I know you know by now that ya nigga Murda, done got a bitch pregnant. Jokes on you now. Hahahaha. But fuck all that shit. I just wanted to drop you a few lines and let you know what's up. You might need to think about taking me back.
Love Ya Baby daddy.

It was only 7:30, so I had enough time to send this muthafuckin' dead beat a response. Nigga had me fucked all the way up. I quickly opened up the other letter to see that it was a Christian mail from a church from Texas.

"Lord forgive me for what I am bout to spit to this bitch ass nigga," I said, grabbing my MP3 player, a pen and some paper before I took a seat at the desk in the room. I searched for the right song, 'cause I needed this nigga to really know what the fuck was up and that I was still that bitch.

Ayo Fuck Boy,
Artist: Jeezy
Song: Can't Ban Tha Snowman

Nigga, you got me fucked up! I don't give a fuck if they reading this shit. Fuck the police! Nigga, FUCK YOU! Can nan nigga stop me, nigga, you forgot who helped you? Me, hating on you? Fuck outta here. What is there to hate when it comes to you? Nigga, all you wanna do is get high and go to jail. What you like something in that bitch that keeps you going back? Nigga, don't come for me. They might lock my body up, but know this, they'll never be able to trap my mind, pussy. Niggas know what kind of bitch I am, Last of A Dying Breed. I am glad that QBanga ain't shit to you, so now I can move how I want to with him, hahhahahah, real talk, nigga. You can't stop shit, just reminding you. You ain't nothing but a pussy ass woman beater that gets high on BOAT. Called yaself coming for me, nigga, you really forgot who I am. So, let me remind you who the fuck I am. I am that bitch, the one that flooded the streets, the first bitch to really have an old school sitting up like a bus, nigga. I made crack different colors, bitch. Had you so mad that you went to the PO on me, you forgot, huh? And you think I am tripping on a nigga getting another bitch pregnant? Come on, nigga, you SHOULD know me. I am the GOAT of this shit, nigga, a bitch ain't never down and can't nan nigga bring me down. I change lives, bitch! Nigga, I would never even fuck you with someone else's pussy. I'll kill myself before I get back with you. You better worry 'bout that shit you got going on, and make sure you keep it a stack, bitch! Cause everybody knows ya bitch ass can't do no time!!!

I was so mad at the response from the court that I took my aggression out on that bitch ass nigga. Fuck the courts and fuck that nigga. I sealed the envelope up and dropped it off in the mailbox.

"Better days are coming," Ms. Kanell said to me after the count was cleared.

"I know it will, but till then, I'ma stay with my head up." I climbed into my bed, praying for better days.

Jamaica

Chapter 15

Murda

I had been visiting my brother every Friday for the last month. "Bruh, I am telling you, that nigga, Antwan, said that you had just given him the work and when y'all got popped, he took a break to make sure muthafuckas wasn't on his ass." I rapped to my dawg behind the glass.

"Yea, that nigga good for the bread. He one hunnid, fam. He always comes through, and my situation won't stop him from his word."

Seeing my blood in an orange jumper with dark brown slides on his feet crushed my heart but seeing a smile on his face eased my sadness. "What about that nigga, Voye?"

"Mane, I have been looking for that nigga since shorty gave me all the information." I studied his eyes, 'cause they were the only thing that really told me how he was feeling. From what I was seeing, he seemed at peace, but a real nigga always knew how to hold shit all the way down.

"Don't worry that nigga will show up, bruh."

"But on the flip side, Dre, Juicy, Lil Bruh, all came through with that bread. The lawyer should be down here next week to see you and shorty," I expressed.

"Have you talked to her?" he asked, referring to Flow.

"Naw, she hasn't reached out, but I made sure she had a band on her books." I know she was dealing with a lot of shit, 'cause this was her second time doing this shit. But she was solid.

"Thanks, bro."

"No need to thank me," I said, leaning mad close to the window. I placed the phone on the desk and mouthed to my blood. "Shit doing good, yo." He bopped his head, letting me know what we were on the same page. "I'm back fucking with the plug from New York."

"Why?" He voiced and I dropped my head. I picked the phone back up.

"Come on, my nigga, that other shit can't hold things down. You forgot that A-Town on the run, and that shit ain't gonna last forever," I shook my head from side to side, "I gotta make sure he's straight!"

"Respect!"

The fifteen minutes flew by super-fast that we didn't move until the officer opened his door.

"Love you, nigga!" I voiced.

"Love you, bro." He tapped his chest and I swear a tear almost rolled down my eye.

***

Shit was moving at a good speed, so I had to be extra careful with these streets. Smoke was standing beside me as we tossed the White Girl around the city naked.

"I am telling you, bruh, we need to cook this shit up!" He declared as we were on the way to make a play.

"Mane, cooking that shit up is way too much."

"You scared?"

"Scared?" We both laughed in unison. "Come on, bruh, you know, I am not scared, I am prepared!"

The more and more I thought about the game, the more and more I saw that I was heading deep into it.

"There goes that nigga, Voye, right there," I said, pointing in the direction of the car wash on Park Avenue.

"Yea, that's that nigga, right there." Smoke glanced in the direction whipping the car around.

"Ayo, what's cracking, nigga?" I hopped out of the car; my pistol was tucked away in my side. "I know you seen me blowing up ya phone and shit, yo," I said, walking up on the nigga.

"Who you talking to?" He looked around, registering that he was the one that I was gazing down like a hawk.

"You know who I am talking to." I touched my waist. I saw Smoke walking from my peripheral. "I need that bread that you owe my brother." I stood in his space, lifting my shirt up. I wanted him to comprehend what I was saying. "And I need all that shit, nigga." I said through gritted teeth. Niggas were posted up, but I wasn't worried 'cause I knew my nigga, Smoke, had my back one thousand. "Dawg, I need that shit today, fuck that shit, I need that shit now!" I pulled the hammer from my waist sticking it into his side. I had a few inches on him so my position was perfect.

"All this is not needed," he whined.

Niggas blew my high with that fake gangsta shit, at first this nigga was trained to go but as soon as I stuck the hammer in his side, he bitched up. "Ol' pussy ass wanna be gangsta nigga, let's go!" I let the nigga climb in the passenger seat as I took the driver side over. "You can take me to the bread, or to the grave yard." That bitch lady luck was on my side, the fucking keys were in the ignition. "Fam, follow us!" I said to Smoke.

"Mane, I got you. I just gotta call someone to bring it to us."

"I don't give a fuck who you call nigga, just make sure that shit correct," I said, pulling out the car wash.

"Mane, I got you," he said, pulling his phone out his pocket as I drove.

"And don't try no funny shit, either, nigga." I poked him with the hammer. I checked the mirror to make sure Smoke was behind me and as I expected, my nigga was on my tail. No room for a nigga to slide between us.

"Ayo, tell Shawn to bring that bag of money to the car when I pull up."

"Make sure that shit is straight," I said, turning on his block.

"It's gonna be straight," he mumbled. His voice expressed nothing but fear.

Two niggas were standing on the front porch when I pulled up. My eyes stayed more on the niggas than they did on Voye. I was ready to hit anything moving in broad daylight.

"Mane, all that pressure ain't needed, yo. You can relax, you 'bout to get that bread."

"Pressure? Relax? If ya bitch ass would have reached out to me, then this would never have been a problem!" I jammed the burner deeper into his body.

"Alright, alright," he whined.

"Shut the fuck up. Call and tell that bitch to hurry the fuck up!"

The nigga did as he was told but didn't get through, 'cause shorty was on the way to the car with a black duffle bag. I put the window down, and smiled at the bitch.

"Is this the bag that you wanted?" She lifted it up and placed it through the window.

"No," he mumbled and before he or she could say another word, I pulled the fuck off, leaving tire marks on the concrete almost running over his bitch when he tried to reach for the door handle.

"Mane, you ain't gotta do all this shit. You got the bread now yo, so we should be good."

I didn't say a word, I drove past the U-Haul knowing that I couldn't' stop there, they had way too many cameras posted around the building. I made a right at the light, and then the first right into the alley behind a youngin's crib that I knew very well.

I slammed the car in park and snatched the bag from his hands.

"That shit is way more," he said when I took the bag.

"I don't give if a fuck as long as it's more and not less, you'll live. But if this bitch is short, I am coming back for ya whole family pussy!"

Bop! I shot the nigga in the leg after I said what I had to say.

"Arrrrrgggggghhhhhh!" He hollered out in pain, grabbing his leg.

"And if you even mention my name, or say a word," I put the Glock to his head. "Ya kids and momma won't live!" I hopped out the car and walked backwards towards Smoke.

"Niggas think this shit is game, fam," I rapped to my homie as we took off to handle our business. From the glance inside the bag, I knew we had way more than he had owed.

"Niggas think shit is a game. We 'bout to turn the heat up on this city," I said, mugging the streets of Lynchburg down, "making them think that Love was still free!" I placed the hammer on my leg.

It was trap time!

Chapter 16

Qbanga

Word around town that the nigga, Murda, was moving and pushing heavy shit, and according to the streets, him and Love was no longer an item. I asked baby girl like two times about the circumstances and every time she dropped the subject. *"That's nothing major for you to lose sleep over,"* was always her comeback. Ever since we had been vibing, baby girl kept a smile on my face the entire time. Her personality was just as beautiful as she was. That shit had me stuck. Hearing her laugh, brought joy to my soul. It was the simplest thing that she did on a daily basis.

"Good morning, I just want you to know that I am thinking about you, and I pray that your day will be great," or, *"Stay strong, stay safe but most of all, stay ten toes down G."* And my favorite one of all time, *"You are hella handsome, and don't let it blow ya head up more, :) have a great day."*

I had been around Love more than Murdoc, but I never noticed how sexy she sounded when she spoke until we started chatting. The way she said my name was mind blowing, she had me wanting to blow the prison up just to get her out. Fuck waiting on them to release her. Baby girl had a nigga's mind on a different level.

The phone call from Ms. Julia fucked my thoughts up. "Hello," I answered, putting my hoodie on to make some moves.

"Hold on, son, your brother on the phone and he wants to talk to you." she said before she clicked over.

"Yo. What's up with you?"

"I'm glad that you called, I need to run something real important across you. I'm not coming to you on no scared shit, 'cause you already know how I am. I'm a real nigga first and foremost and that will never change. I'm rocking with Love."

"My baby ma, nigga? My fucking baby ma, nigga? You my fucking brother, nigga?"

"Brother?" I questioned with a laugh. "You wasn't thinking that shit when you was fucking that bitch I was hitting, huh?"

"That bitch just a bitch, bro," his tone dropped.

"Yea but she was *my* bitch, not yours!" I snapped back. "But fuck that shit, I am letting you know what's up!"

"Nigga, you think I am 'bout to let that shit slide when I land, nigga!" His voice went back up.

"Nigga, see me when you touch, pussy!" I deaded the call on his bitch ass. I was never scared of that nigga, and I damn sure wasn't about to start.

I hit the Corrlinks icon on my phone so I could shoot my baby girl a message.

Beautiful, how are you doing? I pray that your day is going well without any drama and that your head is above water like it should be, 'cause diamonds shine bright all the time. Anyway, I spoke to that nigga, Murdoc, and I told that nigga straight up that I was rocking with you. Nigga said some shit that I am not worried about and you shouldn't either. Anyway, enough with that irrelevant shit, how are you feeling? How was your day? I am 'bout to link up with a few of my G's, so I wanted to touch base and let you know that you are on my mind, hard body, baby girl. HMU later if you get a chance.

***

My trap phone rang and I was ready to chase that bag. "What's up?" I answered, walking to my stash spot in the crib. "I need a block," the caller said.

"Where you at?" I asked, reaching under the bed and grabbing the shoe box with the dope, scale, and sandwich bags.

"At my house," she responded.

"Give me a few, I'ma slide through." I deaded the call and bagged what she wanted and some extra just in case I got more calls. Shorty was asleep on the sofa when I walked into the living room. I didn't want to argue with her, so I tiptoed out the crib.

I made it to Stephaine's house in less than ten minutes. She was already sitting on the porch, waiting for me to arrive. I pulled into her driveway as my personal phone rang.

"What's good with you, G?" BankRoll said. I blew the horn and waved Stephaine down from her seat.

"Shit, I've been waiting on you to link up so we can chop it up." Stephaine was at the passenger side, I handed her the gram and she tossed me the bill. "I thought you was 'bout to let that shit slide, my G."

"My nigga, it's so much to this shit, fam," he expressed. I tapped the console and Stephaine stopped. I said called me with sign language. She nodded her head and walked off. The older white lady was good money, had been fucking with her for a few years, ran across her through one of my G's.

"You not gonna believe half the shit that I am 'bout to rap to you, fam."

"Shit, I expect the unexpected at all times, G."

"I'ma just let that shit be with them, fam."

"What? You gonna let that shit just be, fam?"

"Yea. But know that nigga is no longer apart of the development."

"I knew that was going to happen, niggas don't play that disloyalty shit in this bond. But what are you gonna do 'bout shorty?" I knew deep down my nigga still loved his wife. That shit would never just walk away just like that.

"I might toe tag her my damn self, bruh," he said but I knew deep down my nigga was just talking on his ego and the fact that niggas all around the Burg knew about it.

"If you need help, you already know I am only a phone call away, G."

"Oh, I already know. if there is one nigga that I can count on, QBanga, it's you, my G. Death before dishonor, my nigga, real talk."

"Already, G."

We chopped it up heavily about some major moves that we wanted to make but a huge problem popped up. "How you know that nigga, Murda?" I asked him.

"That nigga been all through my hood acting like it's his shit, G."

Jamaica

"Word?"
"I'm not feeling that shit, my nigga, homie gotta go!"
"I agree!"

Chapter 17

Love

"Ms Jenkins!" Mr. Black, the compound officer, came into the beauty salon yelling. "Love!"

"Yes!" I took off my cape walking towards him.

"You are needed in the unit team office area."

"Right now?"

"Yes, they called for you."

I walked to the reception desk and advised the clerk that I would be back as soon as I was done with what I was dealing with.

"It's cool for me to go across the compound, even though it's closed?" I asked the compound officer.

"Yea, you good to go."

As I walked back to the unit, I made sure my Khaki uniform was tucked in the proper way, I didn't want an incident report for not following their rules. I wasn't really thinking any negative or positive, shit I was just going with the flow.

When I got to the office, the clerk told me to stand by the door and she would call me inside when they were ready.

"What are you doing here?" Shonda asked me as I stood next in line, she was behind me.

"Black came and told me that they wanted me up here."

"I had a call out for team today, so this shit should go by fast. I'm ready to get the fuck in the shower, so I can get ready for House Wives tonight."

After five minutes of waiting, Linda walked out with some white paper in her hands.

"What did they want with you?" I asked, waiting on the clerk to call my name.

"Team," she replied, walking away, and then it hit me. I didn't check the call out for today. I took off after Linda, almost knocking her down.

"I'm sorry," I said, racing to the officer's station to look at the call out that was posted up at the window.

"Jenkins," I whispered my name over and over as I searched the list. "My name ain't on this bitch." I walked back through the doors to find out that Shonda had gone through to the office.

"Ms. Jenkins?" The clerk called my name and I popped my head inside. "They are doing team right now, and I think she was the last one. Yes, she is the last one. They will be with you in a minute."

"Thank you." I stepped back outside and leaned my back against the wall.

It was almost yard recall and I prayed that someone would bring my belongings if they had closed the yard, 'cause I damn sure didn't want to leave it there, it was shit that I needed in my bag.

Minutes passed as I stood still, I wondered what my kids were doing? How were they feeling about me being gone all this time. How would they react to me in the end. Would they respect me or reject me for choosing loyalty over their lives.

"Jenkins, you are next," the secretary said, as Shonda walked past me.

"Thank you." I opened the door with a smile on my face. "Hello, Mr. Black said that y'all wanted me?"

"Yes, go ahead and take a seat, Ms. Jenkins," Ms. Burks said. Mr. Brown was scrolling on the computer across from us at the table. I tried to see what was on the screen but I was blocked by a very dark tint.

"So, you put in a transfer to go closer to home?"

"Yes, I did. And you told me the last time when we talked that it was going around the compound to be signed off on."

"Correct," she said, pushing a sheet of paper over to me. "You are approved to be transferred."

I read over the paperwork. My name, ID number, address where I caught my charge at, my charges, were all correct, so I signed off on it.

"Do you know when I will be leaving?"

"I am not sure, but it won't be that long. Do you need a packing slip to let you know all the things that you can take and cannot take?"

"Yes, I do."

She handed me the paper and that was that, I stepped out the office with a huge smile on my face. I was on my way closer to my kids and couldn't wait. The FCI lifestyle was over for me, it was camp time, baby.

I hit the email station up, to inform a few people of the news. I sent the message to Ms. Julia and QBanga and dipped to make it back to work so I could get my stuff. It was about to be recall where all the jobs for the day would be closed, except for the library, the kitchen and the Rec.

***

The moment we were locked in, I broke the news to my bunkie. "I am getting transferred."

"What?" She looked up at me from her paperwork in her lap. "They making you?"

"No, I am ready for a change, and plus I want to be close to my kids. Hopefully, I can get to see them, if not, I won't be there long."

"Love," she teared up, "I'm going to miss you, so much."

"It's all good, time and location won't change anything." I reached down and hugged her. She was damn sure a great bunkie to have and I know the next person that graced this room will be happy to have her.

That night all kinds of thoughts ran through my mind. I was ready for the fresh start either way. The more I moved around in the system, the easier my time got. Moving made the time fly by fast. This was my second prison and WV Alderson would be my third.

I started selling some of my things and other times, I would just give them away. I was only allowed to have two boxes paid for by the FBOP and if I wanted more boxes, I had to pay for them myself. And it was priced by the weight.

"You know I am leaving, too, right?" Asia said as we were walking to the computer station.

"What? For real?"

"Yes, I am tired of this place. I'm just ready to go."

"Do you know where you are going?"

"Yea, we're going to the same place, but I might go first, though."

"'Cause you been approved for a long time, right?"

"Yea."

I couldn't wait to get the fuck up out of here, no more closed doors, no more five- or ten-minute moves, no more hollering from these wack ass wannabe officers 'bout lock down.

Chapter 18

Murdoc

I called my second baby mother and she was pissed the fuck off, that I had got jammed up.

"I have been calling ya phone for the last damn hour, nonstop," she said as soon as she accepted the call. "What the fuck you locked up for now?"

"They talking 'bout some shooting and eluding the police, I ain't got no bond either! This shit is crazy."

It's been a month and between my baby ma and my side bitch, I was straight. Shorty on the side knew her place and she played it well. I had left her with about 45 bands, so she was handling shit for me.

My baby ma on the other hand, always had her hand out, and even though she knew I was locked up, she didn't give a fuck, as long as her pockets were laced, she was gucci. That's what really made me step out on her ass. Plus, she was sneaky as fuck.

Even though my side joint got on my nerves, I can truly say that she was my down ass bitch for the time being. She handled everything that I asked her to do, and all that talk back shit she did when I was free, she didn't do it now.

"How are you doing?" she asked me one night as we were kicking it on the phone.

"What you mean? You asked me that already."

"I know that, but how are you holding up, mentally?"

"Shit, I am good, blessed to know that you are here doing this vacation with me."

"Already. I miss you, baby."

Her comment caught me way off. Out of all that time that we have been messing around, she never once told me she missed me. My mind raced but all the negative thoughts went out of the window. She could have just taken off with my money, but she stayed grounded with everything.

"I miss you, too, and I want you to know that I am sorry for all the hurt that I caused you," I poured my heart out to her. "Thanks for holding shit down for me, yo. No lie, I can't tell you how much I appreciate all that you are doing for me." I went all the way out with the icing on the cake. "You mean the world to me, shorty."

"You talking that jail talk real good, Tamaine."

"It ain't no jail talk. I'm telling you from my soul."

We talked the rest of the minutes away freely, no argument, it was like we had just met. Shorty gave me a smooth vibe and for the first time in a long time since I had been caged up, I smiled. When the phone beeped, I knew we had less than sixty seconds.

"I'ma call you tomorrow."

"Ok, I'll be here waiting. I love you."

I didn't know what was happening, but I prayed that it was nothing but blessings from above from ol' girl.

"I love you, too." And the phone hung up.

I hit my mom's line and as always, she picked up. "How are you doing?"

"I'm good, just got in from the grocery store," I heard the kids in the background, talking trash to each other.

"Tamaine I am telling you, you gonna make me knot ya head up," Tameia told him.

"How are the kids doing?"

"They good," she replied and it sounded like I had called at the wrong time.

"How ya husband doing?"

"He's good," she kept her responses small and direct.

"Let me talk to one of the kids, Ma."

I heard her telling Tameia to get the phone.

"Hello?" She sounded just like Love.

"Hey, baby girl, what are you doing?"

"Helping grandma get things together, hold on." She had put the phone down. Seconds turned into minutes and all I heard in the background was talking about where to put things at. I had called at the wrong time, so I hung the phone up.

I knew my mom was tired of me getting locked up and I figured my kids were, too. Every time, I got out and tried to do right by them something stayed happening and I would fail. My mom would keep them away from me, telling me I couldn't see them.

"You come over here all the time high as Bobby and Whitney so no, I am not letting them go anywhere with you."

"They my fucking kids, you can't keep them from me," I screamed at her.

"Yeah you right, they are yours! And if they were so much yours, you would stop getting high and get your life together!"

"Fuck you!" I told her in front of my kids. Mad and high as *fuck.*

Damn, I needed to get my life together, fast.

Jamaica

100

Chapter 19

Murda

Niggas had no other choice but to respect my game and get with the flow or test my gangsta and find out just how hard I went in these streets. I heard rumors around the way 'bout niggas trying to rob me, but none came close or even made an attempt.

Even though Love had cut me off completely, I made sure her kids were still straight, her words meant nothing to me. I sent her money monthly, but fuck the rest. I wasn't going out my way to chase her down, I said that I apologized and that was that, but she wasn't having that shit at all.

"Mane, I just heard some shit, that you are not going to believe," Smoke said as he placed the paper towels on the counter top for me. "Bruh, that shit fucked me up."

"What?" I grabbed the bag of ice from the sink, dumping it into the Pyrex bowl. "What you heard that's gonna fuck me up? 'Cause you should already know only a few things can get me off my game." I continued doing what I was doing, paying close attention to the amount of cold water I was adding to the pot, since I had ice already in it. I didn't want the baking soda taste to be on the cookies.

"Love fucking with some nigga named QBanga."

I swear I heard the nigga's words, 'cause my movement decelerated all the way down. Love messing with another nigga?

"Hell no!" I jumped in her defense quickly. "Fuck no!"

"Bruh, I am telling you that shit is crazy. I still can't believe that shit, fam."

"She's messing with who?" I asked to make sure I was hearing correctly.

"Some G'd nigga name QBanga."

"I know who the nigga is."

"What?" He looked at me surprised that I knew who he was rapping about.

"Yea, the nigga her baby daddy's step brother." I dumped the water off the cookies, holding the rest of the unmelted ice cubes back.

"Huh?"

Fam was lost, so I updated him on everything that was fact.

"Damn!" Smoke said, watching me closely. "Nothing with hurt bitches surprised me."

I damn sure wasn't going to reach out to her since she had moved on. My cash flow to her was going to stop, the only thing I wouldn't stop doing was for her kids, but other than that *fuck that bitch*!

I jumped right back in my kitchen mood, that shit was nothing to phase me. I had other shit to do. "It's all a part of life, fam. I'll never let my mistakes hinder me with someone's emotions."

***

"Mane, I'm not 'bout to sit on this bitch and debate with you over how much you're gonna pay me, dawg." The nigga, Zay, from White Rock hit my line bout some work. "Dawg, listen to me, I stand on my shit, toes in the dirt." I packed the sandwich bags up.

"Murda, all I am saying is that shit is way too high, my nigga."

"Too high? Nigga, I am stamping and defending my shit, if you can't pay it, it's cool. Other niggas will appreciate the real fya, my nigga." I deaded the call. I hated when muthafuckas put on a front claiming that they were ballin' but in all, they were flexing hard body but hurting. I am not popping back and forth with no nigga over my supplies. Get it or leave it.

"Ayo, what's good, my nigga?" Antwan said, when I answered the phone.

"Shit, you already know, trying to chase this bag and stuff it down."

"I got that bread for ya brother and I need to holla at you."

"Where you at, homie?"

"Tinbridge Hill, my nigga."

"Give me like an hour and I'ma swing through."

"A'ight, but bring me a cake of that fish that you served for lunch."

"Fifteen," I hit back.

"Bet!"

As I got the streets what they needed ready, I couldn't stop thinking about Love. Shorty had my heart on lock. Would smoke a nigga behind her, give her my heart if she needed it, but this new shit with her, had a nigga ready to tap her head for fucking trying to disrespect me.

I pushed that fuckery with Love to the backseat as I hit the streets. I didn't need my emotions to get in the way with my street hustle. I had to stay focused 'cause it was mad cold out in that bitch.

I tapped into Antwan's line the second Smoke turned on Federal Street. "Ayo, I am turning down the Hill now."

"Come all the way down to the turn around and you'll see me on the corner."

"Bet."

Homie had my brother's money and the money for the work that he wanted. "Mane, this shit looks like straight butter, yo." He held the bag up to the light.

"That's fya, my nigga." I counted the money out that he passed me.

"Oh, fam, it's all there," he said, watching me.

"I understand you, but I gotta make sure, my nigga."

Homie hopped out when I said shit was one hunnid, and he let me know that he would be reaching out to me to cop some more shit, as soon as he had that gone.

My phone jumped with sales, as I traveled around the city making moves until I ran out of what I had on me.

"My nigga, what's good with you?" Antwan hit my line, as soon I walked in the crib three hours later, "I need a fresh bird."

"A whole bird?" I questioned.

"Yea, it's not for me, though. I'ma introduce you to the nigga when you land."

"Who is the dude?"

"Oh, my dawg from the Rock. My homie one hunnid, bruh. His name is BankRoll."

The name didn't ring a bell, so I let homie know that I would hit his line as soon as I reached his spot.

"You know a nigga name, BankRoll?" I asked Smoke.

"Naw, why? What's up? Do I need to get black down?"

I had to laugh cause my nigga was serious as fuck, too. "Relax, killa. He just wants a brick, that's all."

"Oh, 'cause you already know how I am packing, fam," he pulled the 9mm and 45 from his waist.

"I already know," I said, reaching into the stash, grabbing the bird that was needed.

Chapter 20

Qbanga

Antwan advised us that the nigga, Murda, was on his way. I didn't ask the nigga how he knew Murda. I left that shit for BankRoll to do, that was his nigga, not mine. I knew of the nigga good enough. The homie, Antwan, seemed cool but he was not a GD so I was already skeptical of the nigga in the first place. I didn't deal with niggas unless they were in the organization.

"You said that shit was straight, right?" BankRoll asked the youngin'.

"Yea, that shit dat, fam."

My hammer stayed glued to my side, so I didn't have to worry about a nigga having my back. My baby was solid and one hunnid with me no matter the time, or location. As we waited on the nigga, Murda, to pull up, we blazed a blunt of that Hail Mary together. BankRoll rapped with the nigga as I kept my eyes glued to the streets.

Being on Federal, especially in the Hood of Tinbridge Hill was deadly. Niggas was really 'bout that life down this bitch. A young nigga named Sk1p was a little legend in the making and I heard if that nigga heard you was in his hood without permission, shit was liable to go to the extra mile, with someone leaving in a body bag. I hated being in someone's hood and not feeling secured, so once BankRoll told me we were on the way there, I tucked my baby in my jeans.

"How much longer did ol' boy say before he would be here?" We had been waiting for like almost an hour.

"He said that he would link me as soon as he was turning from the main road."

Twenty minutes passed and the nigga was a no show. The sun was setting and I hated being out in the dark, especially in a hood that I didn't know well.

"Hit that nigga again," BankRoll told his nigga.

Then we heard homie's phone ringing, "This the nigga right here, G."

"Yea, I am at the same spot, turn on that turn around and hit the parking lot on the right. I am leaning on the black Charger."

BankRoll handed the nigga the bag of money. "It's all there, right?" The nigga asked and we both busted out laughing. "You said the nigga charged 15 for an ounce but if you bought the whole thing, he would only charge you 37.5, right?"

"Yea, that's what he said."

"Well, it's all there!"

I watched as the car turned the circle and I spotted the nigga first. He was sitting on the passenger side. Antwan was already outside the car with a Macy's bag in his hand.

BankRoll's seat was pulled back but mine stayed up. I didn't give a fuck if he seen me or not, he knew who I was and I knew who he was. Love was the only thing that tied us together, well not really, she was no longer his, but mine.

The nigga pulled right beside us. My hammer was in my hand, with my trigger finger on the trigger. Antwan got into the back seat and I watched closely as Murda leaned forward.

Boom!

Our eyes locked. I didn't turn my face away, 'cause one thing about me, no nigga scared me or put fear in my heart. I watched as his mouth moved and his head turned to Antwan in the back seat. A smile was spread on his face. I wanted to wipe that shit clean and turn it into something stiff.

BankRoll tapped me leg, "Not now, my nigga. Not now."

The moment I saw the back door open, I stepped out the ride, with the pistol in my hand. Antwan looked at me confused.

"Shit good, my nigga," he said, opening the back door to the ride. He didn't know the link that me and that pussy, Murda, had in common.

"Oh, I know shit good, my nigga." They had the window down, so I know for a fact that Murda heard me, I had said it loud enough. "Pussy nigga ain't 'bout shit!"

***

We dropped Antwan off at his spot, he never asked what all that was 'bout, but I could tell that he wanted to, he just didn't know how to.

"Bruh, you good?" BankRoll asked me, as we traveled to his crib on Taylor Street.

"G, I am always good," I kept my eyes on the road.

The product was definitely good, according to the fiend. "That shit that shit," the fiend said, rolling his eyes in the back of his head.

"On the scale of one to ten, how good is it?" BankRoll asked.

"Oh, it's a twenty!"

I looked at my G knowing that what's understood didn't need to be explained.

"Yea, G," I nodded my head as Boosie's song *Don't Know My Struggle* played in the background.

According to the scale, everything was correct. And from the fiends, shit was great.

"We gonna get that nigga!" I bumped Boosie louder and zoned.

Hard times, me and you getting' blisted
Got a dime bag, but we couldn't buy the Philly,
Walkin' to the weed dispenser, we was short on the special.
So we got drunk, snatched purses, man it's whatever.
Old niggas tried to shortstop, we baller blocked, fuck it.
Got a big knot,now I'm thuggin' wit a big ugly somethin' on my waistline,
Bouncin' through the south side
Back then, it was straight gin, Dickies, and cowhides.
You ain't from our side, we bustin' at ya, that's the rules...

Jamaica

Chapter 21

Love
Alderson WV

Two weeks after I had the talk with my case manager about my transfer, before they called my name to R and D to pack my belongings out. I ended up having four boxes. The two extra boxes cost me a hundred and sixty dollars for both boxes, which I paid full in stamps.

My celly was sad and so were my friends, people that knew me, came by that evening to tell me how they wished me the best on my journey and to keep the faith alive. It was bitter sweet, but I was ready for the change of location. I would be closer to my kids and it was possible that I would be able to touch them, physically. I couldn't wait.

Morning came quickly and the list of all the inmates that were packed out, were called to R and D at 6:30 a.m. My bunkie and my friends walked me across the compound to my destination.

"It was a blessing to meet you, Love." Ms. Kanell wrapped me up in her arms. "I pray that God will protect and bless you abundantly, Love." I felt her tears soaking up my shirt. "Stay strong and keep fighting for your freedom."

I pulled back, and smiled at her, "Thank you and I am praying that they set you free, also, so you can get home to your daughter. Stay in the word. God will make a way,"

I hugged her one more time, before I moved around to hug all the people that were there to see me on my journey.

"Jenkins!" The officer came out screaming, "Miller, Stevens, Hall, Harris!" I looked at her and said my name, "Jenkins."

"You have your ID card?"

"Yes," I said, waiting to hear what she wanted me to do.

"Step inside." She moved out the way and I walked through the door never looking back.

Aliceville, Alabama was history to me. I was never coming back. As we were waiting in the holding room, they called us one by one and searched. We were then given new clothing and to another cell we went.

"How many times, they gonna move us before they move us out of this bitch?" Bre said.

I leaned my head against the wall, just ready for this shit to be over with so I could just be in West Virginia.

They shackled my hands first in front of me, then wrapped a chain around my stomach, clipping it to my hands and then cuffing my feet. That shit was crazy. Animals got treated way better.

"How the fuck am I going to walk?" one girl asked. And the officers' come back had our mouths wide the fuck open. *"If you can't walk, we will carry you!"*

Once everyone was chained up, we walked in a single form line out the door and onto a big bus. Officers with guns were standing close by and for a quick second, I thought about making a run for it but took it back when I saw the officer grilling me, closely.

"This is some fuck shit!" I said, trying my best to climb up in the bus without hurting myself.

A bitch ass nigga had me going through this fuck shit. If that nigga would have just held his mouth shut, none of this shit would have been as bad as it is. Nigga got jammed up and instead of manning up, he straight bitched the fuck up and told everything that he knew.

"What's your name?" An officer asked me as I got onto the bus. *What the fuck?* I thought, just staring the bitch down. "Jenkins."

"Your whole name and number."

"Love Jenkins, 16692."

"Yea, yea, yea, move to the back." She cut me off after asking me to say my shit. These muthafuckas needed to get a real fucking life, this controlling shit had me wanting to flip the fuck out.

"How the fuck you gonna ask me my name and number, then tell me *yea, yea, yea*?" I said, walking to the back of the bus shaking my head.

"Love, where are you sitting at?" Destiny asked me.

"Fuck if I know," the seat beside her was empty so I took a seat.

"This shit crazy, right?"

"Crazy ain't the word."

Once the bus was loaded up with all of us. The officer spoke up. "Don't be yelling or screaming on the bus. There is a bathroom at the back of the bus. No, we are not talking off your shackles or handcuffs for you to use the bathroom. You can and will figure it out, if you really need to go."

I looked over at Destiny and she was in tears. "I hate how my life is," she cuffed her face in her hands.

"Lunch will be served on the way out the door to the plane. Any questions?" When no one said anything, she closed the cage and locked it.

To get my head clear, I said a small prayer silently. *"God, I am telling you, this right here, oh, mane,"* I shook my head from side to side. *"Give me strength."*

Destiny didn't say another word, she stared out the window the whole way. Chattering could be heard but I was thinking about my freedom and my kids. Fuck everything else.

After about an hour and thirty minutes of driving, we pulled up at an airport. It was privately owned. No names or signs were around, but little small ass planes. As we looked out of our windows, other prisoners were already there, standing in lines.

"I'm tired of this shit."

"'Bout time you said something," Destiny said, laughing.

I couldn't help but to smile. "Let's get ready for this shit."

The moment the bus came to a haul, the cocky ass officer stood to her feet. "As you are leaving the bus, say your name and number and grab a bag."

"Again!" Someone yelled from the back of the bus.

"Fuck!" I dropped my head.

One by one we came off the bus saying our names and grabbing a brown bag. An officer was at the front of the bus waiting. "Name and number?"

I leaned my head to the side and closed my eyes saying my number.

"Move to the left."

Jamaica

***

We were surrounded outside by marshalls, police officers, and staff members as we waited in the chilly weather as buses pulled up with other inmates, males and females. The males were searched and patted down before they went up on the plane.

"Love, look to the left." Destiny whispered by my neck. My eyes traveled in the direction she said. "What the fuck did he do?"

There was a man with no arms, and no legs in a wheelchair. "What the hell?" I wanted to see how they were going to bring him up to the plane 'cause it was his turn to go up.

Four officers took to him, each on each limb. They lifted him up and took off up the flight of stairs of the plane. My mouth hung open and so did others. *But what the fuck did he do to be in prison with no limbs*, I wondered.

Once all the men were on the plane, it was the females turn. Name and number as soon as we reached the front door. A marshall was waiting for us, telling us where to sit. The females sat in the front with marshalls all over and the men were right behind. Marshalls walked the plane nonstop, making sure the men weren't sneaking trying to talk to the women. But with 350 men with like 20 women, that shit was hard to control.

"Put your seat belts on!" The pilot said. "Make sure your hands and arms are inside of your section at all times!"

Destiny was sitting directly in front of me. We both were in the window section.

"What's ya name, shorty?" I heard a male's voice.

"Don't talk to the females! I repeat, don't talk to the females, and if I catch you, I will put you between a person that hasn't taken a shower in a week and one with a breath so bad that you'll scream."

Laughter could be heard all over the plane.

Once the plane took off, shit got real. The air had to been on high, 'cause it was cold as fuck. I couldn't wait to get to Oklahoma. I was ready for a shower and a nice bed. Fuck this brown bag with peanut butter and jelly with two slices of bread and a plastic bag of water.

Oklahoma was the transfer center; there we would find out where our next destination would be if we didn't know. I prayed that I wouldn't be there long.

"Love, you good?" Destiny turned her head to the window.

"It's fucking cold."

"I know," she said, turning her head around just as the officer was approaching.

When the plane stopped, I was waking up. "Unfasten your seatbelts and remain seated." The command was given to us. One by one, we got off the plane, the women were first this time. Name and number had to be repeated before we walked almost a mile to get to check in, where they had six footprints.

"Step up, walk to the end and stop!" A bald headed marshall screamed.

Six inmates were allowed on the stand at a time. An officer was behind us, as one stood in front of us as they removed the chains from our bodies.

"Females all the way to the bottom and turn left," another officer screamed.

We were stripped from head to toe, squatting and coughing, while pulling our butt cheeks apart. "This shit right here," I said, standing naked beside seven naked females waiting to be given our clothes.

Within four hours, we were taking the walk upstairs to the female section. It was already lock down when we got to the unit. Inmates were seen standing in their doors.

"Listen for your name and your room number. Once you hear your name and number step forward and grab a bed roll and go to your room."

"Fuck!" I said, bobbing my head like I had headphones on. Music was constantly playing in my head. Music kept me going through this storm.

***

Me and Density ended getting in the same room. I was on the bottom and she was on the top.

"I am glad that we are cellies."

"Yea, me, too."

Oklahoma was just like Aliceville when it came to the structure and the rules: they had lock down, emails were stationed in the center of the unit, there was no commissary, and the only ones that worked were the laundry girls. And they got paid nothing.

A day later and my name was called to pack out, I was on my way back to the plane but only to be going to West Virginia. Density was sad, but she knew how this shit went, she had been down for a minute.

"Be good, Love."

"Destiny, stay out of trouble and don't be tricking up your good time, 'cause you gonna need them days." I preached to her before I walked out the door.

"Alderson, West Virginia," here I come, I said to myself as I got on the plane and took my seat.

Chapter 22

Murda

"Pussy ass nigga ain't 'bout shit!" That was QBanga's remark that I heard when I was pulling out of the parking lot. I didn't respond, not that I didn't want to, but there was a time and place for everything. I had another whole chicken on me that I needed to drop off, so that shit he was spitting was nothing compared to the bread that I was collecting.

"My nigga, how that shit happen, yo?" I called Antwan to see what's up.

"What are you speaking on, my nigga?"

"How did you link up with that nigga, QBanga?" I shot straight to the point.

"Oh, I don't know that nigga like that, fam," his tone was low and believable, so I listened closely. "BankRoll, hit me up and asked me if I knew someone with some fire 'cause his people were still out of town. I told the G *yes*, but I never said your name until we were in the car waiting on you."

"Word?"

"On my life, my nigga. But I did ask BankRoll's homie what was up, but the G never said anything to me, so I left it as that."

"It's all good, fam, I was just making sure no funny shit was going on."

"Hell naw, my nigga, you can ask ya brother 'bout me, my nigga. I am one hunnid!"

Maurice did vouch for the nigga, he said that homie was as solid as they came, but I reminded him that it didn't matter how shit was, dude didn't owe me no loyalty.

"Murda," Maurice told me when I asked about fucking with Antwan, *"That nigga is real, and if he's loyal to me, he's gonna be loyal to you."*

I was stamping my brother's words, but if that nigga was wrong, his homie would have to pay the ultimate price. *Death.*

"We gotta handle that pussy ass nigga, bruh," Smoke said to me, as we were making moves. It was something that I had added to my to do list to take care of, but I needed to get word to Love to really find out what the fuck was going on. It didn't matter how hard I tried to get her out of my head, she had a way of getting to me.

"Yea, I'ma handle that shit, fam. No pressure. But in the meantime, let's chase this bag."

After running back and forth across the city supplying niggas and the streets what they had been missing had a nigga beat.

Smoke said he was calling it an early night. He needed to spend some quality time with his wife, since she had been at work putting in long hours at the shop because he was out in the streets with me.

"Just hit my line when you get to the crib, fam." I tossed a bag at him.

"Already, my nigga." He looked at the bag before looking back at me.

"I eat, you eat, my nigga." I was once told from a female that, *"If you feed niggas from the same plate from you, they will protect you more than envy you."* Damn, I was missing Love.

My crib was lonely as fuck, the pictures of Love around the house didn't brighten it up like it used to. Shorty held a spot in my life that no one could replace. I fucked something good up with my dick. *Damn.*

I hadn't spoken to Kandi in a minute, so I decided to reach out as I looked at the picture of me and Love on the wall.

"Hello?" she answered on the third ring.

"How are you doing?"

"Good, just getting fat," she said, laughing. "Baby got me wanting to eat everything up."

"How is Marley?"

"He's good." I heard slow jams playing in the background, I wanted to ask what that was all about, but she wasn't my woman. "Hold on here he is."

"Daddy," I heard nothing but love and excitement in his voice for me.

"How are you doing, son?"

"Listening to Mommie sing around the house."

My little nigga let me know that he was doing hella good in school and he was thinking about joining a sport in school. "What are you gonna try out for?"

"Probably soccer."

"Soccer?" His answer shocked me, I thought it would have either been basketball or football.

"Yes, I just like that sport, plus they be making mad bank." With that answer, I busted out laughing.

"What do you know about making mad bank?"

"I want all that money that you have," his words had me sitting straight up. My son was paying attention to me. I needed to be more careful around him.

"Yes, I work hard every day, so you have to do the same thing."

We chopped it up for a few more minutes until his mom wanted to get back on the phone. "So, when are you gonna come back up this way?" The music in the background died down.

"I'm not sure, but I'ma send you some bread, though."

"The money is not a problem. I just want us to spend some time together, that's all, Martin."

"We will see." I dropped the call. I didn't want to go back and forth with her. We would have never made it off the phone. Jae's picture hawked me down and for the millionth time in the day, she ran across my mind again.

I hadn't done this in a long time, so I grabbed a pen and paper, turning on some tunes. I had to write baby girl.

Love,

How are you doing? I know I fucked up. I can't take that shit back; I just have to wait till I can prove that the baby is mine. Yes, I am asking for a blood test, and if it's mine, I have no choice but to step up and raise that baby, too. I get that I fucked up, but that fucked up email that you shot my way was mad disrespectful, yo. I never called you out of your name. I didn't give up on US, I fucked up, and I am asking that you forgive a nigga, matter of a fact, I am begging you to forgive me. Then I am hearing around town how you fucking with the GD nigga, QBanga. Wowwww, that's all I can say. You dropped me 'cause that nigga spitting game? 'Cause that's the only thing he might have up on me. You know my credentials, so that game shit is out the door for me, especially when it comes to you. The real question is, when did y'all start talking? And it makes me wonder, was this shit on the low all this time behind my back.

I miss you, yo, no lie. You the woman that I need, and I'll do whatever to make you see that, so you already know how I'm carrying that news that I am hearing.

That's all I had to say, nothing more was needed, Love knew who I was, and she knew what I was capable of doing. I had to hear it from her mouth that she was really done with me, and that she was messing with that nigga.

It was nearly 2 a.m. when I got into the shower. I was half way done when I heard my phone going off. "Fuck!" I let the hot water run over my body quickly as I made a dash for my phone.

"Hello," I snapped, using the towel to dry my body off.

"Bruh, where you at, yo?" A-Town's voice barked in my ears. I heard the urgency in his tone.

"I'm at the crib, fam. What's good?"

"Mane, I need a ride!" he said, breathing hard as ever, "Niggas thought that I wasn't gonna clap back, these pussy niggas got the game fucked up!" His words bounced off the wall as I got dressed.

"Bruh, where you at?" I asked, putting my Timbs on.

"Over here on Old Forest Road, behind the Walmart."

"My nigga, I'm on my way."

***

Mane, the moment I saw my nigga walking, I pulled over and picked him up.

"Bruh, fuck that shit!" he said, getting in my car, "Take me over there to the BP gas station, bruh."

"What the fuck is going on, my nigga." I pulled into the Brookside apartment complex.

"Bitch ass nigga, Swap, wanna pull up on me talking mad shit 'bout how I hit his nigga up."

I watched as my nigga checked the chamber as I stopped at the stop light.

"Pussy nigga got me all the way fucked up, fam. That nigga don't know me!"

"You just let me know what you want me to do and I got you, fam."

"Just take me around that bitch, I'ma blaze anything moving, fam."

"My nigga." I placed the heater on my thigh, showing my dawg that I came prepared. "I am riding with you, dawg."

I parked the car right there at the entrance to Brookside. "We gonna walk over that bitch, my nigga."

"Say less."

I pulled my hoodie up over my head, as we crossed the street at Shell gas station. A-Town wrapped a black shirt across his face as we headed towards the apartments across from Biscuitville.

One unit light was on as we entered the complex. Nothing was moving but the sounds of the crickets. "What apartment, fam?" I whispered, pulling my heater from my waist. I rather get caught with it than without it.

"By the dumpster, to the right."

"You ready?" I asked, popping one in the head.

"Been ready, fuck these pussy niggas!"

I heard him checking his gat as we took off up the stairs.

Chapter 23

Murdoc

My wife acting stupid as fuck, but it's because she out there putting on for the next nigga. I was once told: *"The same way you get them, that's how you will lose them!"*

I met my wife through her first baby daddy. Me and the nigga, J, used to chill and smoke blunts daily. He wasn't my best friend, but he was someone that I spoke to regular around the hood.

When he caught his charge, his baby ma, now my wife, used to come around and chill. I didn't pay her any attention at first but as time went by, I started to see and look at her differently. And over a period of time things changed. She left her baby daddy and started fucking with me.

Now that I was locked up, I felt the pattern was about to take place with me and her. But it didn't matter as long as I had a rider on my team, I was good to go. Shorty on the side was still rocking and even harder than before. I never had to tell her to put money on the phone or on my account. She made sure I had letters on a regular with some extra special flicks. She had stepped up more than my very own wife.

"I am not trying to hear that shit, Tamaine." Our daughter could be heard in the background crying. "Every time you get locked up, you wanna tell me how much you love me and you miss us, but when you out this bitch, I can hardly get you to answer the fucking phone." She chatted away bitterly. "Don't worry about what the fuck I am doing, as long as our kid is good, then you should be good."

"Really?" I asked in disbelief.

"Yea, really, nigga. Oh, I know all about that other bitch you have too, Yea, I know you gave the bitch all the money but you're gonna wish to God that you didn't."

"What the fuck are you talking about, yo?" I tried to play the conversation off, but she wasn't having it.

"Yea, I know about her and for what I heard, you ain't the only one that she's fucking, stupid!"

Mane, I wanted to snap the fuck off on this bitch, but I had to pretend that I didn't know what she was spitting at all.

"Mane, you trippin'. I am not fuckin' with nobody. What part are you not understanding?"

"Yea, nigga, tell me the sky is purple, and think I am going to believe you."

"Mane, I ain't called to argue with you, let me talk to my daughter since you trippin'."

"Yea, yea, yea, I am always trippin', Tamaine, always trippin'. But don't worry, we're gonna be good over here, I can promise you that. With or without your money."

The second I heard my daughter's voice, anything that I was feeling from earlier went straight out the window. My baby was my pride and joy.

"What daddy's baby doing?" My tone was low.

"Nothing, watching cartoons and eating candy."

"Make sure you brush your teeth after you are finished eating, so you won't mess up your pretty, white teeth."

"Okay, Daddy."

"I love you."

"I love you more, Daddy."

And the operator came on. "You have sixty seconds remaining."

"Give the phone back to your mommie."

"Okay."

"Mane, you need to stop tripping and rock the title that I gave you."

"And what's that?"

The phone hung up. I dialed my side joint's number, but she didn't answer, so I called right back. Still no answer, so I called right back. Nothing.

"You ain't the only she's fucking stupid," my wife's words rang in my ear, my mind and in my thoughts. I tapped the buttons on the phone again, and no answer.

"What the fuck?" I snapped, dialing the number back.

***

I kept dialing the number for almost fifteen minutes and I was ending up with the same results. No answer. So, I dialed my homie's number, and he picked up on the first ring.

"My nigga, you heard from Shorty?" He knew who I was referring to.

"Naw, I have been trying to drop this bread off to her, but she is not answering or returning any of my calls."

"Word?" I asked, feeling played like fuck. "My wife knows about the bitch, yo."

"How the fuck is that possible?"

"Shit! I am in here youngin'. Try to get in touch with shorty and I'ma try and link with you tomorrow."

"Bet dat, my nigga."

I went straight to my bed with many thoughts running through my brain. *I hope that bitch doesn't try to play me and take off with my money.* My wife was on a power trip and when she got in feelings, she used emotions faithfully over logic. I prepared myself to not have any visits or her answering the phone call so I could vibe with my baby girl.

"Damn!" I pulled the blanket up over my head, feeling the heat from the streets.

Jamaica

Chapter 24

Love

It was two of us that were designated to Alderson, as we got onto the bus that would take us to our new spot, I spoke to the other lady. "My name is Love, and yours?"

"Shay," she answered dryly. I damn sure wasn't about to pressure no bitch to speak to me, so I didn't say another word.

There was a male officer that drove and a female officer that sat her fat ass in the passenger seat. "I'm so ready to get off work," the male officer said with his eyes on the road.

"I know me, too," she said, while eating on a sandwich. The aroma filled the bus up and my stomach started talking.

I watched as they drove, listening to the country music that was playing, looking at the trees and taking in the townscape of my new residence. My body ached and all I really wanted to do was use the restroom.

I had been holding my pee from the plane ride, 'cause there was no way I was walking past all those men to use the bathroom. Plus, using a restroom on a plane while shackled down, wasn't my thing.

Within an hour, we were pulling up at a gate, where the female officer scanned her ID at the gate. The gate opened and in we went. As I looked around, I could spot females moving around and then it hit me, that they were inmates. *Welcome to Alderson* the sign read between two well-trimmed brushes.

Intake went quickly, they stripped us down, searched us, fingerprinted us and gave us a pamphlet.

"Before we send you up the hill, we have to give you a TB shot," the nurse said.

"Okay," I said, extending my left arm out to her. She stuck me with the needle, then placed a Band-Aid on the spot. "Be at medical when you see your name on the call out."

"I will," I assured her and out the door I went.

Alderson was full of hills, it had houses all over the bottom of the hill, but they were condemned. At the top of the hill, there was a building for Medical, two tall buildings, A and B units. My unit on my pamphlet was B. It seemed like everyone was posted up outside as I made my way to the unit.

"Love," I heard my name and stopped when I saw Asia coming towards me.

"Girl," I said, hugging her. "How are you doing? You like it here?" I hit her with back to back questions.

"I'm good and I like it here, more freedom," she said, grabbing the bag that they gave me with my blanket. "What unit are you going to?"

"B, what unit do you live in?"

"A-3."

Then out of nowhere, I heard my name again, "How are you doing?"

"Wheat, how are you doing?"

I knew a lot of people, 'cause I used to do a lot of hair on the compounds that I was at before.

"Girl, it's about time you got to camp."

And before I knew it, I was surrounded by people that I had been doing time with. Asia advised me that she would be right back with some supplies for me.

Wheat let me know that we were in the same unit, so we left the little crowd and went inside. "Girl, you gonna love it here."

"Shit, I am just trying to get this bid over with."

As soon as we entered the building, a bench was drilled down into the floor in front of the phones. A podium was directly across from the front of the unit. There were no doors, just units with walls, no more than 5 feet talk. This was an open dorm. Bathrooms were on both sides of the unit, one section had a hair care section, while the other didn't. Overall, the place was clean, but loud.

***

Months Later

It didn't take me long to make my way around Camp Cupcake. I was stacking my bread with the hair game and working in plumbing. I enjoyed learning about stuff that I never thought that I would do, and knowing that I was doing a man's job, boosted my ego to the point of no return.

"What's your name?" I asked the white girl that started working with us.

"Lee, and yours?"

From that very small conversation, we clicked. We went to dinner together when we could, 'cause she was in the RDAP program. We would walk after hours around the bottom track and talk about life.

Lee was only 5ft 3inches, long, blonde hair, hazel- brown eyes and a body to die for. She had a daughter that was twenty and a husband that she cheated on with a police officer.

"A police officer?" I asked shocked as fuck.

As she told me the story about how she got in prison, all I could do was look at her in disbelief. She was solid, real and raw, she didn't care if you judged her. And I liked her for that even more.

"Black people are not the only ones that sling drugs, either." I couldn't help but to crack the hell up with laughter from her.

"How the hell do you keep up in shape the way you do?" I asked her one day as we were waiting in line to check our emails. She was forty and looking like she was twenty-five.

"I work out, faithfully, Love."

I was still working on my freedom, Asia let me know that there was a lady there that was really good with the law. On a late afternoon evening, I got the chance to sit down with her one on one.

"I'll have a document for you to look over in a few days," she said after we had discussed all the information that she needed to know.

Two days later and I was meeting up with the lawyer lady, Ms. Mar. "Did you know that you signed a 11(c)(1)(c) plea?"

"No?" I didn't know shit about the law and the codes.

"A 11(c)(1)(c) is a binding plea," I looked at her confused, so he continued, "A binding plea is when you can't get a sentence reduction."

"Huh?"

"The plea that you signed is a binding plea, any new law that comes out, won't affect you."

"What the fuck?"

"Yes, but the good news is that someone is taking it to the Supreme Court and is fighting for it as we speak." She handed me a white sheet of paper. "I need you to look this over and l let me know what you think about it tomorrow."

I placed the paper in my pocket and went to my unit.

The document stated: The Supreme Court Of The United States resolves the sentencing issue rather a defendant may seek relief under 3582(c)(2) if he or she entered a plea agreement under Federal Rule of Criminal Procedure 11(c)(1)(c) (Type C Agreement).

The Supreme Court ruled a defendant is eligible for relief under 3852(c)(2) when a defendant accepts a type C agreement.

Due to the fact when a Defendant accepts a Type C Agreement the sentencing Guidelines prohibit courts from accepting Type C agreements without first evaluating the recommended sentence in light of the defendant's guideline range.

Thus, making the defendant Love Jenkins eligible for the two-point reduction under Amendment 782.

It sounded mad good, so I didn't question anything else. The next day, I met up with her and told her it was good to go.

Things were going good for me, I was learning and loving my new trade as a plumber, my kids were good, and QBanga was doing his part in my life. Hands down the only thing I was missing was seeing and touching my babies in flesh.

"Ma," I called Ms. Julia. "How are you doing?"

"Did you get the response for these people about visitation?"

"They denied me." My heart dropped and a tear rolled down my cheek.

"Did they say why?"

"I know why? It's from a charge that I had twenty years ago."

"What? Twenty years ago?"

"Yes, it's a malicious wounding charge."

"What the fuck?" I dropped my head as she explained the situation to me.

"They said that we are not an immediate family but if we were, I would be able to visit you, but since I am only related to the kids, I can't get approval."

"It's all good." I leaned my head back, refusing to shed a tear. "I love you and I will call you later."

I went to my bed and cried, I had no one to bring my babies to see me. QBanga had a murder charge, Snow was nowhere to be found and I damn sure wasn't about to reach out to her. I made up my mind, since I couldn't see my kids, there was no need for me to be here in West Virginia. I would put my transfer in for another prison.

Fuck this shit!

Chapter 25

Qbanga

"So, you saying Murda told the nigga, Antwan, that he must meet up with him by himself?" I asked BankRoll to make sure I had heard him correctly.

"Yea."

"A'ight, let the nigga meet up with him, then." One situation wouldn't stop the show from going down.

"Yea, that's what I told the nigga."

Something about that nigga, Antwan, just wasn't sitting right with me. I hadn't had a chance to put my fingers on it, but I knew for a fact that in due time, I would. I hated how BankRoll trusted niggas so hard and pure. Those same niggas that he had so must trust and love for, were the ones that were stabbing him hard in the back. My nigga had a good heart, one that was going to cost him his life one day.

"So, what's up with you and shorty?" I asked, referring to the situation with his disloyal wife.

"Mane, she trying to dead that shit with the nigga, talking 'bout how it was all a mistake and how much she misses and love me and she wants our family back."

"What?" I looked at my nigga, waiting for him to say he is just joking. But he didn't. "She wants her family back?"

"Yea," he dropped his head and I could feel the tension like he was stuck between a rock and a hard place. "She wants her family back."

"Do you want your family back?" I asked the question that muthafuckas would never ask, or was scared to ask.

"Fam, I miss waking up to shorty beside me. I miss watching her sleep. I miss the nights when I come in from the streets and dinner is still hot. I miss hearing her scream my name. I miss seeing her with our daughter, my nigga, I miss her."

I could tell that my nigga was hurting deep. I watched as he blew the smoke out and took another puff. His head dropped on the back of the sofa as he closed his eyes.

"But when I think about it, how many nights was she laid up beside him? How was she looking at him when he was asleep? Did she cook dinner for him on nights when I didn't make it home? Did she scream his name louder than mine? Did she have an abortion those times when she said she couldn't stop bleeding? Did she love the nigga like she claimed that she loved me?" He puffed again on the blunt and for a long minute or so, my heart ached for my nigga. "Did she really want our relationship back or was she embarrassed that the streets knew how fucked up she was?"

"My nigga, fuck that bitch and fuck that nigga! Loyalty is a must. And death before dishonor should always be that, G!"

I would be a bitch made nigga if I didn't tell my G the truth. I'd always keep it a stack with fam, nothing or no one could change my character when it came to my loyalty.

"Death before this dishonor!" My G said, but I knew my nigga was hurting. That word love was a bitch, you either had to fuck her right, or lay that bitch down.

We discussed how we were going to handle that bitch ass nigga, Murda, in full details. "If that nigga kids gotta scream for him to show up, they gonna scream!" I said before pulling off.

Later that day, I got an update from Love. Baby girl was in West Virginia and according to her, security was tight for me to even slip up in that bitch. *"They do background checks from when Jesus was a baby."* She told me over the phone. Her sense of humor was a plus for me, even though she was down and out, she kept a smile on my face.

"Fuck it, we can still do the skype life, baby girl."

"I mean yea we can, if you want?"

"If I want? Come on now. I've been dying to see your face, and your smile, *Love*."

"Alright, I'ma set it up for us this weekend."

"Why can't you do it today?" I asked ready to see her.

"You have to set it up four days in advance, and you have to accept it before it expires, too."

"Mane, I'll never miss it, baby girl."

We talked about her day and just listening to her talking about plumbing had a nigga's pride on swoll. She knew how to do a lot of things most niggas didn't know how to do. One thing about her, no matter what she was going through or the location, she never allowed the time to do her, she mastered everything she got her hands on in that bitch. When the phone beeped, the smile on my face disappeared.

"I'll hit you up sometime this week," she said.

"Shit, you better hit me up on the email when you get up."

And we both laugh. Baby girl had that magic to her, and I couldn't wait till I could get my hands on her. A nigga was in heat.

***

Tonight, was a direct go. Niggas wanted to act like their actions wasn't going to get touched but in life there was always a time for everything. Karma never hits you right back, it takes time and just when you are on the rise, here she comes with a bucket of shit to dump all over you.

"Where that nigga live, G?" I asked, driving the buckie that we got from the pipe head.

"Over there in the Meadows."

"We can't just drive up in that bitch, fam," I let him know right off top. "I'ma park on the left hand side by CVS since there is a little short cut through the bushes that will take us directly to the first building where the nigga supposed to be at."

"Bruh, I just want to take the moment and thank you for having my back like this, G," I listened to BankRoll, never interrupting his words. "Niggas, be quick to say how much they are for you and with you, but as soon as you ask them to ride for you, it's an excuse. Niggas are only around when life is good, they are there to see what they can learn and what you can give them, but when it rains and the mud is piling up, they run, never looking back on the good times that we had."

I turned on the street that CVS was on, I hit my lights and let the car on. Once I was comfortable with the spot of the ride, I pulled my mask down over my face, then I put the black gloves on one by one. I checked my tool, everything was straight.

I looked over at my nigga. "No need to thank me. If the shoe was on the other foot, I expect you to be there for me, just like I am here for you. Niggas can say whatever comes to mind, but when you show that your actions can back your words up, that's all that's needed." I cocked the hammer. "Life is never always going to be good or great, and it damn sure ain't 'bout to rain all the time either, but know this, whatever you do in life, or whatever you plan on doing, know that I am always going to have your back no matter what, right or wrong. I am riding with you, G. We grew up together and I don't mind dying with you, my nigga!" I opened the car door and stepped out into the dark night.

"Let's party!" BankRoll said as I led the way through the dark bushes.

Chapter 26

Murda

The light from the hallway flickered like it was about to blow. I watched as A-Town pointed up the stairs. We had one more flight to take.

"First door on the right," he signaled.

I wondered how the fuck were we going to make it in that bitch. I looked around, making sure no one was near in sight. As I looked off the tier, I spotted headlights from the parking lot.

"Somebody coming," I whispered, tucking my heater under my hoodie. We leaned against the wall, like we were chilling, but no one came our way.

Boom! Boom! Boom!

A-Town beat against the door, but no one answered. So, he banged again.

Boom! Boom! Boom!

Still nothing. He tried the knob, but it was locked.

Boom! Boom! Boom!

I leaned my ears to the door, hoping I could hear someone on the inside but nothing.

"This shit is a dead-end, fam." I said, stepping to look over the railing. "Ain't nobody here, bruh."

We hit the stairs, two at a time. "I know them niggas round here, fam."

"If you think they're around here, let's play the waiting game, fam." I said, tucking the hammer back under my hoodie into my waist.

"Fuck that, them pussies knew what I was 'bout," he said, walking back towards the entrance. "Ain't nothing 'bout me scared, my nigga."

For a split second I thought I heard something behind a car moving, so I stopped walking, placing my hand on my hammer.

Blocka! Blocka! Blocka!

The shots rang across my head, I dipped my head down, never allowing my feet to stop moving underneath me.

Blocka! Blocka! Blocka!

I let my toolie spit back. "Fam," I heard A-Town's voice throughout the shots. "Yo!" I ducked behind an ol' school Chevy.

Blocka! Blocka! Blocka!

The gunfire continued. I wanted to lift my head up but I didn't know where the shots were coming from so I stayed low.

Blocka! Blocka!

More shots were fired. Then I saw a few niggas running towards the building that we had just left from. I jumped up and aimed.

Blocka! Blocka! Blocka!

I fired. Niggas were like lightning with their feet.

"Fam!' I heard A-Town's voice behind me, but I kept busting at the niggas in front of me. "I'm hit, my nigga!"

"Where you at?" I glanced around the parking lot, trying to locate him. "Fam?" I searched between a row of vehicles, looking behind my back to make sure the niggas never came back. "Fam?" I stumbled into a nigga on the ground, leaking. He was looking up at me with his eyes wide open.

Blocka! Blocka!

I sent two more shots into his body before I went to search for my family.

"Bruh? A-Town?" But I didn't get any answer, so I kept looking for my nigga. There was no way I was going to leave without my nigga. Dead or alive, we came together and we were leaving together.

"Bruh?" I turned around to find my nigga squatting down holding his stomach.

"I'm hit, my nigga, I'm hit." He gritted in pain.

"Where at, bruh?" I asked picking him up. I tossed his arm over my shoulder as I placed his body on my body.

"I'm not sure," he mumbled. "I'm not sure but I feel the burning sensation."

I limped with my nigga all the way to the main office of the complex. "Stay right here," I slid his body down the side of a car. "I'll be right back." I dashed across the street and down the road to Brookside. My lungs screamed for air, but I was on a mission to get back to my nigga. I had to. I needed to.

With my heart beating and my heart racing, I started the car and put the metal to the floor.

"Bruh?" I picked him. "Bruh?" I voiced but he didn't respond. My nigga's eyes looked up at me as I laid him in the backseat of the car. The car light's glisten in his pupils. "I'ma get you help, my nigga."

I pressed the gas as I raced to Lynchburg General Hospital. "My nigga, stay with me." Damn, I couldn't afford to lose my nigga at all. Not now, not ever. The streets were empty as I hit each curve about 60 miles per hour.

"Ughhhhhhh!" my nigga moaned out in pain. "Brrrrruuuu," he muffled and it hurt my heart to the core hearing my nigga in pain.

"Fam, don't worry, we're almost there!" I hit the pedal to the floor as I made the left on Tate Springs Road.

I pulled right at the front door, tires squealing with the pressure from the brakes. I hopped out the car and made a run for it through the front door. I was hollering by the time I got to the front desk.

"I found this man bleeding on the side of the road!"

"Calm down, sir," a nurse said to me.

"He's in my car." I ran back to my car. Once I got there, I hurried, "Bruh, they are on the way out here to get you. Where is that joint at?"

He tapped his side. I flipped his body over and I heard the loud moan that escaped from his mouth.

"Sir," the nurse said.

I dropped the hammer on the ground and helped ease my nigga out the car, placing him in the wheelchair that they had brought outside for him. I slammed the door and locked eyes with my nigga. Our eyes spoke volumes. Loyalty was that and more to us.

"Sir, we are going to need information," one of the nurses said.

"Let me park the car and I'll come and talk to you."

I got in my car and said a prayer to God above. *"I know we run these streets likes it nothing, too many G's and real niggas are already up there with you. I am begging you to help my nigga pull through. Real niggas die, but please don't let that real nigga die."* I left the parking lot with tears running down my face.

Thugs cry, too.

***

"Smoke!" I screamed into the phone the moment my nigga picked up. "Bruh, I need you to come to my crib, right now!"

"Say less, my nigga. I'm on my way!"

I reached in the back seat as I drove trying to find the burner on the floor but I couldn't place my hand on it. "Fuck!"

How the fuck did the night turn out like this? I had to clean shit all the way up. The car would be seen on the video, they would identify me coming in the hospital from the cameras. "Fuck!" I punched the steering wheel. "Gotdamn!"

As soon as I got to the crib, I changed my clothes. Putting the bloody ones in a trash bag. And hitting the shower for a few minutes. I advised Smoke that the door was unlocked and he needed to get here fast.

I was out of the shower in a blink of an eye. I started packing all the money and drugs up as the water from the shower dripped off my body. "Fuck!"

"Murda," I heard Smoke's voice from the front door.

"My nigga, I am back here," I moved into the closet, throwing some clothes on.

"Bruh, we gotta get this shit out the crib." I tossed him a few duffle bags.

"Say no more."

Chapter 27

Murdoc

I was wide awake before the lights came on. "What's good with you, yo?" The white boy, Kool, asked me. "You good? You gonna go to breakfast, if so, are you gonna eat ya boiled eggs?"

"Damn, it's 6:25, yo, and you asking me a million and one questions dawg," I stepped around him and headed towards the phones. They came on at 6:30 a.m. and I didn't want to wait in a line. I wanted to be the first one there.

I picked the phone up and glanced at the clock, it was that time. I dialed Shorty's number so fucking fast, that I fucked it up, so I had to do that shit again, but this time slower. I wiped the handset of the phone on my orange jumper as I prayed that shorty answered the phone.

When the call went unanswered, I dialed her number right back. And on the second ring, she picked up. I waited for her to press one and when she did. All the anger I had for her last night went out the window. "Hey, baby, how are you?"

"Good," she answered in a comatose tone.

"What time did you go to sleep last night?" I made up conversation just not to snap the fuck off on her.

"Uhmmm," she yawned, "I left my mom's house late as fuck. And you know when I am over there, I don't have any service . So if you called me last night and didn't get me, that's where I was."

"Yea, I called but I figured you were sleep."

"How are you doing?" she asked and all the unexpected feelings that I had last night were no longer there. Shorty gave me peace and hope during this tornado.

"I need you to holla at the homie for me, he got something for you, bae."

"Okay, I will as soon as I get up and get myself situated."

Hearing the sleepy moan that she was making had my dick jumping. I had to hold my dick down inside my jumper.

"It's the same dude, right?"

"Yea, and you meeting him at his crib." I felt relieved talking to her that I didn't realize I was saying too much over the phone, until I heard her coughing. It was our code to let each other know that we were saying too much information on the prison phone. "Yea, yea," I played it left. "Did you mail them pics off for me yet?"

"Naw, bae, I am going to do that shit today."

"Promise?"

"You know I got you."

We rapped about how her family was doing, and she explained to me how she had planned to spend a few nights up there to help her mom, since she had just come home from the hospital from having a stroke.

Our conversation flowed easily as we listened to each other. Shorty knew about my wife, according to what I told her. I made sure to dog my wife out to her, making her know that she was about to take her spot.

"Fuck that bitch, boo. I wish you were the mother of my daughter."

"In due time, we can have our own child."

"Big facts, baby. Big facts." I let shorty know that I would hit her later after dinner. She was cool and blew me a kiss through the phone.

No one was waiting in line, so I hit my little nigga's number up. "My dude. What got you up so early, my nigga?"

"You know the early birds get the first worms, my nigga."

It was something that I taught him when I took him under my wing. *"You must stay on your grind, collect everything, even pennies, my nigga. Money adds itself up when it has you as a machine behind the grind."* And my words stuck with him because he was doing exactly what I told him. *"Determination and motivation get you where you want to be, and only you can be that determination and motivation to yourself to collect that bread."*

"Shorty gonna hit ya line when she gets herself right, homie."

"Bet, plus I got some extra cheese for her too, dawg."

"Already."

There was nothing more to be discussed, so I dropped the call and hit my wife's line, but the bitch didn't answer. So, I hung up and went to see the nigga with the library in here.

"What kind of fire books you got that I can read, my nigga?" Homie was mad cool, he would let you read his books for two stamps per book.

"I got the series by Meesha called Renegade Boys, it's four parts to that shit and they're straight lit."

"Bet! Let me get them and what else do you have after I finish these joints?" I held the books up.

"All the books. I got the hook up from Lock Down Publications, 'cause that nigga is killing the book game right now."

"Alright, I as soon as I'm done with these I'ma check everything that you have by that nigga's label."

"Bet."

"And bring me the payment when you get it."

I had to laugh 'cause that nigga was 'bout his bread with the books, that's how he made his living. His family sent him the books and he would flip the hustle in this bitch. People that loved to read and didn't have family members to come through for them didn't have to worry 'cause he had the book reading club on lock.

***

I finally got a chance to talk to my wife, and the bitch was still going off. The moment I told her that my homie was reaching out to her with some moola, she shut the fuck up and ceased all that bitching that she was doing.

"Where is my daughter at?"

"Our daughter, you mean?"

"Yes, our daughter," I corrected myself fast. I didn't want to hear her fucking mouth today.

My princess was with my mom, so I knew she was having a blast with her brother and sister.

"Alright, I'ma hit you tomorrow."

"Tomorrow?" Her voice pumped up with fuel to go ham.

"Yea, it's lock down time, babe, chill. I love you." I lied 'bout it being lock down, I just wanted to get the fuck off the phone with her. The love I had for her was creeping its way out the door.

"Oh, okay, I love you, too."

Chapter 28

Qbanga

Running through the woods at night was a great idea, no one expected anyone to come through the woods this time of night. But I am a gorilla, I hunt niggas down through rain, sleet and snow, so the woods were nothing for a monster like myself to travel.

I heard BankRoll grunting behind me. My nigga wanted us to go in from the front, but I had to let him know that I wanted to make it out and live for another day so the back would be our entrance.

"G?"

"What's good, fam?"

"Thank you!" Even in the dark, I could tell that my G was emotional.

"No need to thank me. We family, G. Remember that." The full moon light gave us just enough light for us to see where we were going.

"Plenty Much Love!" he said.

"Never Too Much!"

The path led us down a little hill and all the way to the hallway of the building that we needed to be in. My mask was already over my head. I saw the camera, but that shit was not working according to one of the G's that lived over here.

Not a soul was posted up outside the building that we were in or the one directly across the street. The complex sounded like a graveyard.

Two by two, we hopped up the stairs till we were on the third floor.

"You got the key?" I whispered to my fam.

"Yea," he reached inside his pocket and pulled it out, placing it in my hand.

A little bitch that was the property manager gave us one of the master keys for the apartments. She charged us ten bands but that was nothing compared to what we were about to gain.

I slid the key in and turned it as slow as I could, I didn't want to alarm anyone. My heart was pumping so fast that I thought that shit was gonna hope right out of my chest. My anxiety fueled as I turned the knob and pushed the door slightly, hoping it wouldn't squeak. There were no animals allowed on the property, so that was an extra plus for us.

The instant the door opened enough for me to walk through, I had my jammie out, leading the way. I remembered the property manager's words, *"The living room is first and then it goes right into an open kitchen. A hallway, is right to the left…"* I locked in all the information that she had provided to us.

The floor squeaked and I stopped walking. G was behind me, he too stopped moving. I walked on my toes, heading straight to the main room, my nigga would check the other room out.

The door was cracked open, enough to see that they had left something on that gave out light. Clothes were all over the floor, as I stepped into the room.

Two bodies stretched over the bed. My target was on his back with his arm across the bed as a bitch rested peacefully on his arm. No one moved.

A light snore escaped from shorty, while dude's mouth was wide the fuck open.

BankRoll was at the female's side.

"Pussy nigga!"

I placed the cold steel against his temple. His eyes popped open like a fresh batch of popcorn. Shorty had yet to move.

My nigga's eyes said it all as he looked over at my G standing there with the pistol at shorty's head.

"Rise and shine, nigga." I motioned him with the pistol to move.

"Hmmmmmm," shorty moaned with her eyes open when he pulled his arm from under her. "Arggggg," she screamed, but BankRoll shut her the fuck up.

He had that steel inside her mouth like she was sucking a dick. Her eyes danced back and forth to the nigga but he couldn't do anything. Real niggas were in charge. She clutched the sheet tighter to her chest.

"I need all the bread, nigga. All of it."

"I don't got nothing, yo." He sat up naked as a baby that had just entered the world.

"Nigga, don't try me." I pushed the hammer deeper against his temple. "Move."

He got off of the bed and I gave him enough space to move. I walked with him to the closet never blinking or looking away. Dude was vicious, so I had to make sure that I was on my P's and Q's.

"Don't gag on my shit!" I heard BankRoll telling the bitch. "Keep all that spit in ya mouth, bitch!"

He opened the closet and it was two duffle bags wide open, his head dropped and seeing the cash, my eyes rejoiced. "Pull em out." I pushed the hammer in his back. He reached down to pick up the bag, but chose to swing on me instead, so I let the heater talk.

Blocka!

I hit him in the chest, stepping back. I heard shorty muffling cries. But the nigga didn't drop, so I clapped his ass again, this time in the knee.

"Arrrrghhhhhhhh!" he screamed out, dropping to the floor.

When he dropped, I heard BankRoll's hammer clap. I knew that shit was a straightforward shot in the mouth.

"Pussy, you thought I wasn't coming for you?" BankRoll stood beside me pulling his mask up. "I gave you loyalty, nigga, trusted you with my life, had you 'round my kids, but you just had to fuck my bitch, huh?"

Fools eyes danced back and forth, as blood leaked all over the carpet.

Blocka! Blocka!

He let two off to the head. I grabbed the bags and headed for the door while BankRoll tossed drugs all over the house.

Outside was still silent but I knew that shit wouldn't be long, and that urged me to move faster. Hearing gunshots in the hood this time of night had nosey muthafuckas wanting to see what was going on.

I was halfway up the hill when my G caught up with me, out of breath. He grabbed one of the bags and we literally ran to the car.

"Pussy nigga thought I wasn't coming for him!" I heard him sing behind me.

"One more to go," I said, talking about his wife, "but only if you want to."

Chapter 29

Love

"Love," Lee called my name when she walked into the plumbing shop. "We have jobs today?"

"Hell, yeah. A toilet in A unit and a sink in the precious RDAP unit." And she busted out laughing. "Boss," I yelled to Mr. Anderson from the back of the room. "Me and Lee are about to do those jobs, sir."

"Alright, Jenkins!"

Our crew leader, Edwards, asked if we needed help, but as usual, we denied her help. Me and Lee made a great team, plus our vibe was vibrant, we didn't need anyone around to fuck with our space.

"You ready?" I asked and Lee just looked at me and rolled her eyes. This white girl was a trip, but I had grown to love having her around me. She was sentenced to 36 months but with the RDAP program, she only had to 18 months.

"Girl, I am telling you, I wouldn't be able to do 15 years, Love," she said, as we pulled away from the plumbing shop in the go cart that she was driving.

"Shit, you don't have a choice but to do it, Lee. I damn sure not 'bout to kill myself over no fucking time, either. I love my life, girl."

"Yea, but I am not about to suffer, either."

"Girl, who the hell said that I was suffering?" We drove past the cafeteria.

"I would be if I was facing 15 years, Love!"

"Lee, let's not talk about time."

"Know this, when I get home in December, you will be hearing from me."

So many bitches had told me that and not one had shown me that their word was law. "Lee, I heard that shit before."

"Yea, I know you heard it before, but I'm different."

Lee was funny as fuck; she would tell me stories about her life every time we were doing a job together. "Today's story is from my daughter when she was a little girl," Lee said as I picked the ladder up from the back of the go cart. "Love, I am going to bring the bag, 'cause you know I am skinny and I can't lift that shit like y'all be doing."

Once we got to the unit, Lee announced that we were turning off the water in order to fix the leak from the toilet. I pulled the flop down from the ceiling and looked around for the water main line.

"Lee, flush the toilet and get all that water out," I said, turning the main water line off.

It was a caution sign in the stall, so I placed it on the floor and scooted my ass on it, on my back and under the commode I went.

"So, my daughter gets mad at me because I told her that her friends couldn't spend the weekend, 'cause I had to work on Saturday."

"Pass the channel lock." I cut her off.

"Anyway, I told her maybe next week, they can come over but not this week. That little ungrateful cunt had the nerve to tell me that I was a horrible mom."

"What?" I looked up at her for a second before I turned the knob. Repeating the words in my head, *left lose, right tight.*

"Yea, so you know what I did?" she said, holding the toilet up as I got the screws off. "I went into her room and took everything out of that muthafucka. I didn't even leave her with a picture on the wall."

I was cracking the fuck up under the toilet. White people did extra shit that would make a person kill themselves. Black parents just gonna talk shit or beat ya ass.

"I left her with a pillow and two sheets on the bed. A pair of panties and an outfit for the next day."

"What?" I tossed the screws beside me, not wanting to lose any of them.

"Yea, I am a horrible mom, so I was showing her just that." She laughed and I did, too.

"I know she was mad as fuck seeing that you had done that shit, wasn't she?"

"Hell yeah, cried for days, telling me how sorry she was, but I made her live like that for a week."

"Lee, you crazy as fuck, so make sure you holding this muthafuckin' toilet up," I said, sliding between her legs as she placed the commode on the title.

We got the leak handled in fifteen minutes. Turned on the water and announced that the bathroom was back open. On to the next job we went, thanking God it was Friday.

"What are you doing this weekend?"

"Shit, I got a skype tomorrow with that dude I told you about."

"Ya kids' father step brother?"

"Yup."

"Oh, shit!"

"Shut the fuck up." I said with a laugh.

"Girl, you only live once, so fuck it. What time is your skype?"

"Two and Two-thirty."

"He's getting two."

I didn't respond. I just laughed.

***

I woke up around twelve, made me some tuna with crackers, ate and then I hit the shower. My hair was already washed. All I had to do was flat iron it and get dressed. Time moved as I got right to see my boo thing.

Lee was outside waiting on me, when I walked through the door. "Damn, girl, you got a date with Denzel Washington? You are beautiful outside those big ass plumbing clothes."

"Shut up!" I grabbed her by her arm in a playful way, so we could walk down the hill to the email and skype room.

"How is the family doing?"

"You're not gonna believe this shit I am about to tell you. My fucking husband found out that I was fucking the police officer, and know he wants a divorce."

"What? Did you confess?"

"Well, not yet."

"Lee, you can't tell that man while you are in here, he is going to leave you hanging."

"Fuck him leaving me hanging, his ass don't do shit for me. My sister does it all. So, fuck him!"

White people handled shit different than black people. We was quick to hide shit, had to beat it out us, white people they were going to tell you straight the fuck up. "Yes, I was screwing him in our house, in our bed."

We laughed so hard going down the hill, just enjoying each other's company. Lee was different, she didn't care about the color of the skin, or where one came from or what they did. All she saw was the moment.

"Girl, go in there and blow that man away with that smile," she said as I walked through the door for the skype.

I was nervous as fuck to log in, my hands were sweating as my heart raced. I logged in and he was there, I checked myself out in the little section at the bottom of the screen and then out of nowhere, his face popped on the screen.

"Damn, baby girl, you are still beautiful." His eyes were locked in on me. And if my complexion was white, I would have been looking like a stop sign from all the blushing that I was doing.

"Thank you," I said, smiling so hard, that my cheeks hurt.

He rocked a fresh low waved haircut, a Gucci shirt and a gold Cuban link chain around his neck. He wasn't the little nigga that I used to break bread with anymore. He looked grown up and matured. His pearly white teeth had me dazed the fuck out. Hygiene was a must.

"How are you doing? He sat inside a car with the door wide open.

"I'm good, just chilling."

"Good. You beautiful as fuck, yo!" The way he complimented me had me floating. He made emphasis on everything about me. "Your skin is still spotless."

"Boy you crazy," I pulled my face away from the screen, smiling hard as ever.

"I'm for real, yo," he said when I popped my head back in. "Damn!"

The hour went by fast but the time was worth it all. Before the time ended, he made sure to let me know, "We have to do this every week, baby girl."

"I'll try!"

Lee was waiting for me as I walked out of the room. "How was it?" Excitement danced in her eyes.

"Girl, it was that and more. "I smiled for the millionth time within an hour.

"Good, so what do you think?"

"Huh?"

"I mean you are at a point in your life to know if he's the one or not, friend."

I didn't respond, we just walked the bottom track till it was time for us to return to our units.

"I'm not coming out tomorrow, so I'll see you on Monday."

"Alright." I walked off. My mind danced around me as I moved in the wind.

"Love," I stopped and looked back at my friend. "Stay strong and know that I admire you."

Jamaica

Chapter 30

Murda

A day later and the news reported, "Twenty-seven-year-old Micheal *Mike* Smith was found shot to death in the parking of the 3300 Old Forest Rd. Dave is live at the scene." The news lady disclosed. "Dave here reporting live on Old Forest Rd." He looked around and the camera man showed exactly where they were. "According to witnesses on the crime scene. They heard gunshots late Thursday night, early Friday morning. One witness said that he looked out the window but he couldn't see anything so he got his family on the floor in the kitchen of their apartment. One man is reported dead at this moment. Families here say it's a horrible thing that happened and they are scared not knowing what else might take place. Reporting from Old Forest Road, back to you in the studio."

I looked over at Smoke, my nigga had yet to put fire to the blunt. I hadn't heard anything from A-Town or about my nigga.

"Bruh, you gotta call the hospital, dawg," Smoke said, staring into space. "We have to find out what is going on with the fam, yo!"

We were sitting in the shop with the lights turned off, the only thing that was on was the television.

"I know. I need to find Snow and let her check that shit out."

"Bruh, she might have Facebook," Smoke was thinking now.

"Shit, I don't have that shit, though." I handed him the lighter.

"But I do, though."

I walked back and forth in the shop thinking about life, praying silently that my nigga was still breathing. I rather him locked the fuck up than dead any day.

"I found her."

"Send her a message and drop my number with it, too."

Niggas screamed how loyal they were and how hard they went, but my nigga, Town, was everything that came out of his mouth.

"Fuck!" I reached for the blunt, but I didn't need it, my body was already numb, my brain was moving slow and I wanted this shit to be a dream.

"Got damn!" Smoke's eyes were buried into his phone.

Back and forth I walked.

"Bruh, she's about to hit ya line, she said."

I stopped moving, taking my seat back beside my nigga. "Fam, you gotta chill, yo," Smoke expressed, but I couldn't. I craved to know that A-Town was good.

The ringing of the phone in my pocket, had me standing back to my feet.

"Hello, this Murda?"

"Yea, what's good with you?"

"Shit, you?"

"You heard that shit 'bout bruh?" I started walking again.

"Yes."

I paused dead in my tracks.

"Please tell me that my nigga alive." I closed my eyes. Seconds passed that felt like hours and she still hadn't said a word. "Please say it ain't so." I opened my eyes and a flash of lights dashed in front of my eyes from the main road.

"The hospital called me," she stopped talking.

"The hospital called you and what?" My heart raced.

"They said that he is in intensive care," and I was finally able to breathe. I turned around and pumped my fist in the air. Smoke walked over to me and we embraced each other.

"He is also under arrest for that shit that happened."

"But what about his health?"

"The doctor said that he was going to be fine."

"That's a bet."

"Yes, it's a blessing. I am going up there to see him in the morning, so I will hit your line when I get there or from there."

"That's what's up and thank you."

"No problem."

***

Two weeks passed and my nigga was good. Snow did let me vibe with the nigga, but he never discussed anything and I didn't say a word. My brother was mad as fuck when I told him what happened.

"Nigga is you thinking?" He tried to scream at me during our visit.

"What you mean, am I thinking?" I stood to my feet.

"You out there acting stupid over niggas that's not ya blood!"

His comment crushed the root of my heart. I knew me and A-Town weren't blood, but the loyalty that he gave me made our bond stronger than steel. That nigga always had our backs, no matter if we were right and wrong, so hearing that shit that my brother was spitting made my body twitch.

"You know the meaning of blood, nigga? That nigga put in work for you on different occasions, for us. And you sitting up in this bitch talking about how he's not our blood! This the same nigga that went into a whole shoot out with a nigga that ratted on y'all," I dropped my head. "But I see how shit is," I picked my head up and stare the nigga that came out the same pussy as I and spoke. "Do you know the meaning of loyalty? Cause blood ain't shit!" I dropped the handset and walked out the cube never looking back.

***

December 2017

A-Town was charged with attempted murder with the shooting that happened in the club. The nigga survived but was scared to death to even identify fam as the shooter. But according to the video records, they knew it was fam, so they charged him with all kinds of shit, but that was the most dangerous charge.

They weren't able to link him or me to the death of the nigga on Old Forest Road, thank God. Shit was hectic 'cause I was putting in mad work with the streets to make sure my people were straight. And even though my brother took me off his visitation list, I still made sure the nigga was good. I showed up to each court date that he had, just to let him know that I was there. The truth always hurt. And a guilty conscience would kill you faster than life itself.

Flowsicka was holding it down, nothing came out of shorty's mouth and it showed that loyalty over everything was just that with her. Love didn't respond to my letter and it broke me down inside. Kandi was getting big as fuck and even though she wanted me to hit it again, I turned her down.

"I don't understand how you can come up here and not touch me when I am carrying your child, Murda?"

"Mane, that shit was not supposed to happen, yo." I kept it a stack and straight forward with her.

"How the fuck can you say that, yo!" She raised her voice. Marley, our son was at school, so I let her be.

"Easy, just like I said it."

"What have I done to go through this shit with you?" She rubbed her stomach.

"You fucked that nigga that killed my nigga, that's what the fuck you did, bitch!" Her mouth hung open and I walked out on her.

Chapter 31

Murdoc

My wife left, she sent me the divorce papers and I signed them as soon as I got them. Word through the joint was that she was fucking with another nigga from the hood. I thought the love we had for each other was real but as time passed, she switched up and I did, too, and that made me step out on her.

I got to talk to my daughter because she was steadily dropping her off at my mom's house so she could do hoe shit. I couldn't control her pussy from behind these walls. She was fucking while I was out, so I knew for a fact she gonna fuck while I was in.

"I gotta let that hoe be a hoe," I rapped to my little nigga.

"You can't let that hoe stress you, bruh. I might be stressed out, but I'll never stress over some pussy, bruh."

"Already, little nigga." I knew what my man was saying and I respected it, 'cause it was big facts.

"So, don't be in that bitch stressing over that hoe. We changed the topic and got straight to the money. "But shorty on the other hand been holding shit all the way down for you and I salute her for that shit, my nigga. I ain't heard shit about her out here disrespecting you in anyway, my nigga."

Hearing my dawg's words made me feel good to know that the one that I didn't expect was doing what I needed her to do. Shorty was proving that she was for me and only me.

"I still need you to drop some bread off to my baby mother, though, and my mom."

"Just let me know the total, and I will get on that shit today."

"Twenty-five. Twenty to my mom and five to that hoe."

"Say no more, but on another note, bruh, how are you holding up?"

"Shit, I am good, I got court in the a.m., so I'll see what's good."

"Word," the phone beeped. "Hold ya head, my nigga."

"Already, my homie, and you stay safe."

"You already know. I am strapped up. Always."

***

I was up all night, not being able to sleep had a nigga drained as fuck when they called my name to go to court.

"Good luck, yo." My cousin, Woody, said to me on my way out the pod.

"I thought you had court today, too?" I asked, waiting on the pig to unlock the door.

"Yea, but it's later, at 2:30."

"I should be back before, then," my time was 9 a.m. and here they were coming to get me at 7:45 a.m.

Once I was on the holding cell at the courthouse, I got on my knees and said a small prayer. "Lord, have mercy on the judge today. Amen."

I entered the courtroom with a smile on my face, seeing Shorty in the courtroom made shit so much better for me. Her undying love and support was truly appreciated. And if she rode this bid with me, I planned on showing her nothing but the best.

"Mr. Davidson take a seat," the judge demanded.

After the whole introduction about swearing to tell the truth, I took my seat.

"We call the witness to the stand, Mr. Tony. Please, step forward."

And the bitch nigga did just that. He walked forward, glancing over at me with a smile on his face. The nigga was the nigga's cousin that I had shot. He was there when the whole shit went down. And if he placed me at the scene, it was a wrap for me.

The District attorney got right to work. "Good morning. We've got a high ceiling in here so I want to make sure you speak up. All right?"

Witness: Yes.

DA: Can you please tell the jury your name?

Witness: Tony.

DA: And you're twenty years old, is that correct?

Witness: Yes.

I dropped my head. I knew exactly where this shit was heading. "Fuck!" I mumbled under my breath and my lawyer tapped my leg.

DA: You live in the city of Lynchburg?

Witness: Yes.

DA: Can you tell me how you know Mr. Leonardo?

Witness: He is my cousin.

DA: Can you look in this room and point out anyone that was around that day that your cousin got shot in front of your eyes?

Witness: Yes.

DA: Please do, Mr. Tony.

That nigga looked around the room before his eyes locked in on me. And in slow motion, I watched his hand rise up and then the finger stuck out.

Witness: Mr. Davidson.

DA: No more questions, Your Honor.

That's all it took for them crackers to do me in. We sentenced you to five years for malicious wounding, with nothing suspended Mr. Davidson.

The court asked if I wanted to say something, but what the fuck was there for me to say?

Fuck that snitching ass nigga!

I got back to the pod and hit Shorty's line. She answered on the first ring.

"You think you can ride that wave with me, baby girl?"

"What do you think? Have my actions displayed otherwise?"

"Naw."

"Good, so don't question me again." Her words touched my heart, the whole time I had her as the side bitch, I should have had her as my main bitch.

"Thank you for coming out today to show me a lot of love. I am sorry for all the shit I put you through, yo."

"Tamaine it's all good, I just want you to know that I am here for the long run, through the trials and tribulations, I am here."

I couldn't say shit, 'cause it was the truth, so I poured my soul out to her, "Snow, will you marry me!"

"Yes, I will marry you!"

Jamaica

I knew this shit was about to fuck the streets up. Yea, I started fucking Love's best friend, the day she gave me the green light and I wouldn't change it for anyone. Love thought it was cool with her fucking with my step brother, so she should be okay that I was about to marry her best friend. It wasn't no fun if the baby daddy can't have none.

Chapter 32

Love

It fucked me up when Lee told me that she was leaving in a week. "Love, I am always going to be here for you, know that." "I hear you, Lee," tears formed in my eyes. "I am going to miss you." I held her in my arms.

"I know you heard it all before how people are going to do this and that and don't do shit, but all I can do is show you." She pulled back from my embrace.

"It's whatever," the tears ran down my cheek. "I am about to put my transfer in and go to a different prison."

"Why? You are close to home."

"That shit doesn't mean shit, I can't see my kids in person, only on skype. Everybody got a felony charge, what the fuck I'ma stay here for?"

"I feel you." We were sitting outside the Plumbing shop by the train tracks. "Whatever you do, I am going to be there for you."

The week of Lee's release came quickly. She had to report to R and D at 7am so I was already up and dressed waiting for her at her dorm door. The moment I watched her exit the building, tears raced down my face and I didn't stop them. She said goodbye to a few people before she made her way over to me with a small box. "Who is picking you up?"

"My sister."

"How are you feeling?"

"Bitter sweet. I met some real true people here on this journey. Some will always be a part of my life forever," she was spitting, but her actions alone had to show me different.

The closer and closer we got to R and D, the more and more I got depressed. I didn't want to go to work today, but I knew I had to. Time didn't stop cause my friend was leaving, I had to keep pushing. I came in this bitch alone and I would leave this fuck shit alone.

"Love," she dropped her box at her feet. "I love you, my friend. I can't tell you how you made my time so much easier. There were days when I thought that I wasn't going to make it, but your strength and love showed me I could." We were both crying. "I love you, my friend."

She hugged me again and walked off never looking back. I wished her nothing but the best that there was. She was a real down to earth person, full of life, and had jokes for days. I will definitely miss Lee.

With tears running down my face, I walked my sad ass to the plumbing shop. I had a lot to do today. Two toilets in B unit to fix, a sink in A unit and the chapel needed their drains to be blown.

I didn't go to lunch or take a break. I asked my boss if I could get off early and he agreed that I could. So, instead of getting off at 3:30, I got off at 2. I walked to the email room to check my messages before I got up to the unit, 'cause I wasn't coming back down here for the day to check my emails or even go to dinner.

I logged into my inbox to see that I had a few messages, one from my daughter, one from Bae, and one from Snow. I clicked on my daughter's one first.

"Mom, how are you doing? We are doing good, missing you more than you are missing us. Today was a good day, school is good. Grandma is ok and our little sister is staying with us. We love you mom."

I replied: *"Hey beautiful, I am good, and I am happy that y'all are good. You will never miss me more than I miss y'all. Y'all are my world, my everything, remember that. And I am glad that grandma is doing good. How do you like your sister over there with y'all? I love y'all till the death of me."*

I checked QBanga's message and as always, my nigga knew how to put a smile all over my face with his words. Didn't matter how bad my day was going, he was always there to put a smile on my face. I was really falling for thugga, daily. My next email was from someone that I thought was my friend, but with time, her secrets were exposed.

"Love, how are you doing? I know it's been a hot minute since I reached out to you, but I had and still do have a lot going on and on my plate at the moment. We have always kept it a stack with each other no matter what we were going through, so I am coming to you woman to woman. Months after you got locked up, I have been seeing your kids' father. And before you start going ham, no I never looked at him like that when y'all were together. I know this shit sounds fucked up but I am kinda doing something that we can sit back and laugh about later in life. I love you and I miss you, but you shouldn't trip on this either, 'cause according to Tamaine, you are messing with his step brother. What happened to you and Murda? Here is my new number, HMU. I love you, always and can one change that."

I didn't feel hurt or upset, it was life. Out of sight, out of mind. Loyalty was just a word that people used. What it meant to me wasn't the same definition for the next person. Instead of replying, I deleted that fake ass bitch. Fuck her, fuck my sperm donor and fuck Murda! They all could fuck themselves.

I got to the unit, hit the shower and made me some nachos to eat for dinner because I wasn't going to the chow hall. "Love," I heard someone hollering my name. I was in my room, so I stood in the chair and looked to the top of the unit. It was Mona, the Spanish lady that worked in the laundry shop. "You have a social."

A social was when someone from a different unit wanted you to come outside to meet them 'cause we weren't allowed in other units unless they were on a work detail and there was an emergency.

"Who is it?" I yelled back.

"Asia," she said, walking to her room.

"Thank you," I slid my sneakers on and grabbed my hoodie.

Asia was standing under the pavilion, so I crossed the street to see what she needed. "How are you doing?"

"Shit, okay. How are you doing?"

She came to check up on me since she heard that my friend had gone home today, and to find out when I could do her hair. She asked me if I had heard anything from the courts and I advised her that I didn't.

"Mane, I am ready to get the fuck up out of here."

"What do you mean?"

"I am ready to go to another spot."

"Damn, why?"

"I am just ready for a change, plus I need to stack some bread up."

"Girl, you make enough money doing hair and working, don't you?

"Hell naw. I gotta take care of myself and my kids."

"But don't you have a few niggas on ya team?" She placed her hands on her hip.

"I hate depending on a nigga or anyone, I rather hustle my shit from the dirt, so a muthafucka can't throw shit in my face," I schooled her. We chopped it up for a couple minutes before I went back to my unit.

The next day, I went upstairs to see my case manager to put in for a change of address. I knew a few people that lived in Florida, so I used one of my homies' joints.

"Why do you want to leave?" Mr. Macalister asked.

"I am just ready for a change and I want to be closer to my family." I lied.

"I thought you were from Lynchburg, Virgina?"

"I am, but I am ready for a change, I want something different."

He didn't ask me shit else, but advised me that he would put my paperwork in for a transfer.

All I did was work, do hair, skype with my kids and QBanga. Life was feeling good, even though I was locked but when I heard that the pussy nigga that told on me and the entire city was getting out of jail, I got mad depressed.

"How the fuck?" I asked Qbanga over the phone.

"Mane, that nigga gave the city up and the system respects that shit, baby girl." He said as I cried over the phone. "But know this, your kids can walk with their heads high, and you can too, 'cause you stayed true to the code of life."

"Already!" But all that shit he was spitting didn't change how I was feeling, that nigga was getting his freedom back while I still had eight years left to do. "Fuck!" I yelled when the phone call hung up.

***

Three Months Later

The bitch made, pussy-snitching ass nigga was home with his family, while the rest of us were still caged up. According to a few people that reached out to me from the Burg, they said that Worm was getting mad love coming home.

"Muthafuckas claim they so real, but I guess it's because that nigga didn't tell on them or someone that they love, so it's cool to show that nigga love." I vented to QBanga. "A bitch like me will never tolerate that shit, I wouldn't give a fuck if a muthafucka told on my enemy, snitching is snitching and if I salute that shit, I will fall for anything!"

"Facts."

Lee was home and was doing exactly what she said that she was going to do, riding the wave with me. She sent me cards when she could, but most of all, she emailed daily, and if I wanted anything done, she handled it for me. She had shown me more loyalty than muthafuckas that I knew most of my life.

She was filing for a divorce from her husband. *"Muthafucka was out here fucking the whole time, Love. And wanna talk about how I cheated. I told his ass to sign the papers and we are selling the house, it's over."*

As I was reading her email, I saw her going ham on her husband and it made me smile.

"I gave that muthafucka twenty-three years of my life and for him to think that he can do whatever, he got me all the way fucked

up!" I read her email with tears of laughter running down my face. *"It's Loyalty Over Everything!"* She signed the end of her email.

I updated her on all the things that were happening in my life and I couldn't wait to hear what she had to say.

Chapter 33

Qbanga

"G, you basically telling me that you taking this bitch back?" I asked my nigga, trying to comprehend what he was saying. It seemed like he was talking too fast for me to understand, so I asked him to repeat himself.

"I am going to give her another chance."

"For all of that, you should have let the nigga live, then, my G. You placed our lives in danger for a bitch that you knew you were taking back?" I closed my eyes and tilted my head to the sky.

"Fam, it's a lot more to it."

"A lot more to it, how you figured that shit. This the same bitch that was fucking ya so called nigga, the nigga that you would die for. The bitch that you gave everything to was stabbing you in the back the whole time." I laughed. "And I rode with you cause you my nigga to handle that shit and now you going back to her? So, let me get this shit straight, you gonna tell her that you slumped that nigga, too?"

"Naw! Hell fucking no, my G!"

I got in my car and pulled off. Nothing more needed to be verbalized.

As I traveled home, I hit Phat's line. "My G, how are you doing?"

"G, I was just about to reach out to you, we need to link."

"Where are you stationed?"

"I just sent you my location."

I checked my messages and it was there, "I'ma pull up on you in a few, G."

"PML." Phat let me know it was Plenty Much Love. A statement that we used in our organization when we were leaving or ending a conversation with one of the G's.

"Never too much."

The conversation with BankRoll didn't sit well with me and if that nigga took her back after all that shit, I knew he would pillow talk to her. Letting her know he would kill for her any day.

"Fuck!"

I pulled up at my nigga's crib but instead of me getting out the car, he entered my car. We dapped each other up with love.

"My nigga, you heard the news about Fool?" He shot right to the point. "Hell naw, what happened?"

"Mane, niggas rocked his dome, along with his shorty. The boys found drugs all over the house."

"Word?"

"On my life, G."

"Damn!" I expressed some sympathy with my face.

"But fuck that shit," he lit the already rolled blunt. "I heard that you and some clown named Murda got beef."

"My nigga, you know I don't do that beef shit. I pull up on any nigga trained to go, he just lucky it ain't his time yet."

"Already. I haven't put in any work in a minute so if you need some hands my G, I am here!" He tapped his chest passing the blunt over to me.

"How is the family doing?"

"They good and yours?"

We spoke on the meeting that should be going down in a few weeks here in the Burg. "Niggas gotta be reminded of principles and morals."

"G, that's nothing but facts."

"Niggas need to be reminded that this shit is not a game, and if they not down with the codes of life for this organization, then they can remove themselves."

"Big facts."

Chopping it up with the G let me know that shit was definitely real. The whole time we were chopping it up, I couldn't shake the fact that I had a feeling that BankRoll was going to tell his bitch about what we did to Fool.

Instead of going home, I drove back around to that BankRoll's crib, but as I was about to pull up, I spotted the Benz that he had bought his wife parked across the street, so I kept it pushing.

"Fuck, that nigga gonna sing," I said, turning the block to hit the highway. I had to get the fuck home and think before I did something that would cost me more than I had already done.

"Fuck!" I pressed the gas pedal to the floor.

As soon as I got in the front door, shorty was sitting up on the sofa with a glass in her hand. From the look on her face, I knew the night was about to be hell.

The television blared with gun shots from the Shotta's movie. I locked the door, trying my hardest not to lock eyes with her.

"So that's what we are really doing now?"

I stopped and turned around only to see her standing in a pair of six inches heels with a blue tank top and white boy shorts, my favorite colors. *Damn*, I bite my lip, feeling the pressure swelling up in the head below my waist.

"So, we really not fucking with each other no more?" She was all in my face, her breath smelled like strawberries, her hair hung down her breast. "Can we make this work with us?" Her hands rubbed across my dick. "I need to make us work? We need to make us work?" She grabbed my dick, and it rocked up in her hand.

"I need you," she pressed her body against me. "Please me, even if it's just for tonight," she begged, tipping up on her toes. "All I need is this night," she purred in my ear, "just this night and this night alone. Please just let me help us, please each other." Her lips kissed my chest, my stomach as her hands unbuckled my belt. I gazed down on her, but the way she bit my dick inside my pants, I stuffed her head there on the spot.

My pants hit the floor, as my dick poked out at her in my boxes.

"Hmmmmmm," she moaned as she massaged my nuts. She pulled my boxers down and my dick stood at attention. The moist air from her mouth made my wood jump.

"Ughhhhhhhhhhhhh," and in my dick went. The saliva was warm as her head swallowed my rock. I staggered back but she held onto my calves with both hands as her jaw kept sucking.

My dick was all the way at the back of her throat, , and not once did she gag. "Fuck!" I grabbed the back of her hair, pulling her head back and forth. "Got Damn!" In all the time that we had been together, not once has she sucked my dick like this before. "Fuck!" I looked up at the ceiling and I swear I was looking at the stars.

Her hands released my balls and grabbed both of my ass cheeks. "You know much I missed sucking this dick?" She asked as she licked the head, looking right up at me.

"Show me!"

With each long stroke that I pounded in her mouth, the more she moaned. Her knees were drilled into the carpet, using one of her hands, she stuffed it inside her shorts. The noise that her mouth made on my dick made me want to buss all up in her throat.

I pulled her up by her hair. She tried to kiss me but I pulled my face away from her. "Damn it's like that, huh?"

I ignored her remarks, walking her to the sofa that I came home and saw her on. "You just want a fuck, right?" I tossed her over the arm of the sofa, "I am just giving you this dick!"

She didn't utter a word, she leaned her body over the sofa and pulled her shorts to the side. Face down, ass up.

I placed my finger at her hole, and it was sloppy wet, so I eased my dick inside of her slowly. Her back arched as her head lifted up.

"QBanga," she moaned my name and I rammed her faster and faster. "Yes, yes, yasssssss." She sang and she bounced her ass back on my dick.

"Throw that pussy to me," I said, rocking in and out of her. Leaning her head back, I snatched up a handful of her hair.

"This what you want?" I asked her as I put a hurting on the pussy. "Huh?" But she didn't answer so I lifted her left leg up and placed it on the cushion of the sofa. My legs throbbed but I refused to give up until I was spitting seeds all in her.

I wasn't worried about her getting pregnant 'cause she had the Mirena inside of her. I felt the feeling in my toes as it made its way up to the head of my dick.

"Fuck, fuck!" I dug deeper and deeper inside of her. "This what you wanted, huh?" I ripped her ass cheeks apart making my way to the tunnel.

"Yes, this is what I need," she finally spoke with a tone that I knew way too very well. She was crying.

"Ugggggggggggggggg." I let all the vitamins go inside of her. "Did that nigga fuck you like that?" I said, pulling myself out of her.

"Fuck you! Fuck you, QBanga!" She turned around and tried to swing on me but I grabbed her arm.

"Bitch, get ya mind right." I said, pushing her ass on the sofa. "Raise them muthafuckas again and they will be gone."

Jamaica

Chapter 34

Murda

My brother and Flow's court date was on Monday and A-Town's was on Tuesday at the same time, 10 a.m.

"Shorty, you are a strong, stronger than most niggas that claim that they are strong." Flow reached out to me. "I know that shit is fucked up but you have to hold your head above water."

"My nigga, my head is high, don't get it twisted. I am not new to this; I am true to this. I am more worried 'bout my grandma more than anything. This time that they 'bout to throw at me, is nothing."

I knew what she meant, the time was never a problem, but leaving love ones behind was the hardest and the problem.

"My grandma is getting old and plus she is sick." I heard the pain in her voice. Flow had always been about her family. "Have you talked to your brother?" She changed up the subject.

"Naw, I haven't spoken to him in a while. That nigga was mad out of pocket with a situation, yo."

"For real?"

"Yea, but that shit doesn't stop my love for him, but he needs to understand that life is life and loyalty is loyalty."

"Loyalty?"

"Yea, but don't trip, it's nothing on y'all end. But it's still love."

"I feel you."

We vibed a little before they disconnected the call. I let her know that I would be there at court tomorrow. I had to cancel my trip to New York so I could be in attendance and give support to my family.

"We just gotta make the trip during the week, Smoke."

"Yea, it should be nothing, my nigga."

"How ya wife said the shop moving?"

"Oh, everything going in the right direction. She complains every now and then, but she let me know she will be riding till the wheels fall off."

"My nigga, you got a good one."

"Yea, took me a long time to see that shit, Murda. A very long time. I cheated so many times that I lost count. She found out, took me back, forgave me, but I still stepped out."

My nigga was lucky, most women would have turned their backs, gave up, cheated, probably set a nigga up.

"Got a bitch pregnant, but she stayed with me until we found out that the baby wasn't mine."

"What?"

"Yea, my nigga, I been through it all. That shit you going through now with Love, I was there and did that."

"I see," I got up and walked towards the table, I needed to get shit ready so I could hit the road. Paying for three lawyers placed a dent in my pocket, plus taking care of my kids, Love's kids and sending money to prison was not easy. A nigga still had to eat, run a business and still live. "We've got mad moves to make, fam."

After rounding up the streets and supplying what the streets were calling for, I got a called from a number that I didn't recognize. "Yo."

"What's good with you, nigga?" the voice responded, but it wasn't a familiar tone that I knew.

"Who this?"

"This BankRoll from the Rock."

I heard the nigga's name but I didn't know who he was. New niggas were never welcome to reach out to me, but for the nigga to take it upon himself to make the introduction himself, I knew he had balls.

"Can I link with you?"

I thought about it and it could only be for one thing. "Yea, meet me at Friday's in an hour."

"Say less, G."

It didn't take me long to get to Friday's on Timberlake Rd. I got me a seat in the back, while Smoke sat a few seats behind me. I ordered a Jamaican Lizard and a batch of hot wings.

"Is that all for you, sir?" The server asked, staring me down.

"Yea, for right now." I replied, handing her the menu. "Oh, give me a Long Island Iced tea, also."

"You sure that's all you want?" She licked her lips as her eyelashes flicked up and down nonstop.

"Yea, that's all I want." I slant back in the seat at the window.

"I'll be back with your order," she said, turning around and walking away, but with a meaning. Her ass bounced up and down. For a quick second, I wondered what her pussy would feel like wrapped around my dick. But the thought quickly vanished as soon as my phone went off. I dropped my head back, gave Smoke the code that the nigga was somewhere near.

"My G, I am here." I watched him walk through the front door with his shades on. Two heavy chains hung from his neck and from his appearance, he looked like he was about his paper.

I stood to my feet with the phone still glued to my ear. "Look straight to the right." I spoke into the phone and when he spotted me, I dropped the call and took my seat.

"What's good?"

"What's good with you?" I nodded my head towards the seat across from me.

"Your name is moving weight around here," he moved his finger around in a circular motion. I didn't say a word or move a muscle. "I am trying to link myself in and do business." He stopped when the waiter walked up with my food and drink.

"BankRoll," she greeted him when she had my food and drink down. "How may I help you?"

"Shit, let me get a salad, with the steak combo with a Long Island drink, Jasmine."

"Would you like anything else?"

"Naw."

I watched him watch her ass as I dug into my food. A nigga was hungry.

"Back to the subject at hand, yo."

"As I was saying, I am trying to link a line of connection with you on some major weight." I studied his face as I stuffed my face.

"I know you got that fire, so whatever the price is, I am willing to pay, as long as it remains the same quality that you've been serving the streets."

"How do you know about me?" I asked the question that I already knew the answer to.

"My nigga, Antwan, holla at you for me."

It was facts. Antwan did tell me that the nigga reached out to him wanting some fire and when he told him he could get it and stand on it that it would be just that, he called me.

"What numbers are you looking at?"

"I need 'bout 5 birds, naked, though."

"You need about 5 or you *need* 5?"

"Price for one?" I knew this nigga was QBanga's people. I had seen him that night slouched down in the front seat that night that the nigga, Qbanga, tried to test my gangsta.

"Thirty-eight," I finished up my Jamaican Lizard.

"Thirty-eight?" He looked around the room, before moving his head in closer across the table to me. "You charged Antwan 37.5 for the bird."

I didn't say a word, I didn't owe this nigga an explanation, he wasn't anyone that I needed, he needed me. The extra bread wasn't shit. I dropped a bill on the table and proceeded to get up from the chair.

"Okay, okay, thirty-eight," he said when Jasmine the waiter arrived with his food. I sat back down and continued to finish eating my food.

"Damn," he said once she was out of ear.

"You either go with the game, or you'll get left."

As he ate his food, I set down my laws. We would meet in a private area, or at his crib. He agreed to do it at his house. He would call me a day in advance to let me know what he needed for me to deliver to him.

Everything that I said, he agreed to, no questions asked.

"See you in a few days." I left the bill on the table as I got up. "Dinner on me." And I was gone.

***

Maurice and Flow were given a plea. Maurice got one for thirteen years, and Flow received one for ten. They both hopped on it. Maurice let me know that he would hit my line by sending word with his lawyer. Flow smiled as she walked out the courtroom and even if something was bothering her, we damn sure couldn't tell. Shorty held it all the way down.

Instead of meeting up with BankRoll the next day like we had planned, I called the nigga right after court and told him I would be at his spot soon. I had to throw this nigga off his game, never giving him a moment or a chance to have one up on me.

"I'm outside." I hit the nigga's line once I was around the corner from his house.

"Bet."

I had everything that he had requested. I even had the money machine on deck.

"What's good with y'all." He opened the back door. Smoke didn't say a word, he just kept his eyes in the rearview mirror.

"What's good with you?" I turned around and dropped the grocery bag in his lap. "All five there!"

He handed me a small little bag. "It's all there."

"It's all good, I'ma check right now since we're both here." The money machine was already hooked up and ready. I ran each stack through the machine as we waited. Fifteen minutes later and everything was all there.

"It's all good, yo. Hit my line if you need me."

"I will," he exited the car and we mashed out.

The courtroom was packed as fuck. Muthafuckas from almost every hood was there in attendance. I nodded my head to a few people than I knew before I took my seat in the third row. Snow was sitting right behind his lawyer and where he would be sitting.

Across the room were the nigga's parents, siblings, and his friend that bruh had tried to smoke. I mean mugged the entire opposite side of the room letting them muathafuckas know shit was real, and I was on deck to support my nigga to the fullest.

I heard the door opened and in came a wheelchair with the witness in it. Ohhhh's and Ahhhhh's could be heard all throughout the courtroom as a security guard pushed him on the witness side.

"Pussy ass!" Snow yelled and the lawyer turned around and said something to her.

A few minutes later, my nigga thugged his way in the courtroom, and even though he was caged up, my nigga rocked the orange jumpsuit with a swag out of this world, he had a mild limp and a smile was on his face as he twisted his lip up staring at the nigga in the wheelchair.

A-Town looked over at us, and I saluted my brother. Snow blew him a kiss and a few niggas expressed their feelings: *free you.*

A-Town turned around and said a few words to Snow, and I knew my nigga was relating a message for me with the way she was bopping her head up and down.

Whatever the nigga wanted me to handle, it was getting done. Fuck that shit, that my brother.

Maurice was saying loyalty was a must and everything. I knew if I was in the situation that Town was in, and he was free, anything that would have asked the nigga to do, he would be doing it without any questions.

"Please, rise," the bailiff announced. "Your Honor Judge Dowling's court is now in session."

Once the judge was seated, he announced that the room could be seated. The district attorney got up and walked to the front of the room calling his witness to the stand. The nigga couldn't get up to walk, someone from the DA section pushed him to the front of the room.

"Identify yourself," the judge told him and he did. "You swear to tell the truth and nothing but the truth." The nigga raised his hand and repeated everything that the judge had told him to say.

A-Town's head never dropped, and his shoulder stayed puffed out. His eyes were locked in on what was in front of him. Snow flipped her hair behind her as her body rocked from side to side.

"Can you state your name for the court," his lawyer asked him and he spoke his name up, loud and clear for the room to hear him. "Do you remember the night that you were shot?"

"No, I can't."

"Can you recall where you were on the night of the shooting?"

"No, I can't."

"So, basically, you don't know who shot you?"

"No, I don't."

I was amazed at how the nigga held that shit down. But the real reason was because he knew if he didn't, things were going to get ugly.

"No further questions, Your Honor." The DA stepped to the side.

A bailiff from the other side of the room walked and pushed the nigga back to his section. *No witness, no case,* that's all I was saying to myself, until I heard them called the other witness.

"What the fuck?" I heard A-Town mumble. The jury looked over at my nigga.

And in walked a tall bald-headed nigga in a full black suite with a huge grin plastered over his face. He didn't make eye contact with anyone but DA. A blonde headed lady with mean ass shape for a white woman. She gestured with her hands for him to take the stand and he did without blinking.

"Mr. Bird, do you swear to tell the truth and nothing but the truth." She stood in front of him.

"Yes, I swear to tell the truth and nothing but God's honest truth."

"Were you present on the night that witness was shot?"

"Yes, I was."

"What all did you see?"

"On the night that he got shot," he pointed towards the nigga in the wheelchair before he continued. "The argument started in the club, I am not sure about what, but from the hand movements from both parties."

"Both parties? Can you point both parties out for me?"

The nigga pointed at dude in the wheelchair and his head slumped down, then he pointed at my nigga, A-Town.

"Continue, sir."

"According to rumors in Lynchburg, they got into it because someone had snitched on one of A-Town's people in the dope game."

My bruh didn't move a muscle. My legs shook under me, cause everything that the snitch was saying was facts.

"So, Mr. Town approached the victim and went all up in his face, and before I knew what was really happening, fists were flying."

"And then?"

"Then Mr. Town was getting the best of the victim but he kept striking him until he fell to the floor."

"And then?" She walked back and forth in front of the room.

"Mr. Town stood over the victim and fired shots into his body."

"Did you see Mr. Town holding the gun?"

"Yes, I did!"

"No further questions, Your Honor."

The lawyer that I paid all the money for didn't have a chance, they had the video and they had a witness to point my nigga out. "Court will recess in an hour with the verdict," the judge said, standing up.

An hour later and we were back in court, waiting. The judge read the following words from the document that was handed down to her. "We, the jury, find Mr. Town guilty on all charges."

My nigga didn't drop his head or say a word. Snow wiped tears away from her face.

"I sentence you to 45 years in prison."

My mouth hung open and the court exploded. "Fuck that bitch! Fuck that snitch!"

"Order in my courtroom," the judge screamed, banging her gavel. Once the room got quiet, she said, "Mr. Town, do you have something to say?"

My nigga kept sitting. He looked back at me and smiled; he blew a kiss at Snow before he stood up. "Fuck all ya bitches!"

Jamaica

Chapter 35

Love
A Year Later

I was in Coleman Florida, at the women's Camp loving the summer heat. It was the best move I ever made doing this fifteen-year bid.

"Love, you like it there?" My homie Angela asked me.

The women's prison was surrounded by four male joints. A medium, A low, Pen 1 and Pen 2. The women cut their grasses and if they were on lock down the women were there doing everything for them.

"Hell, yeah. Matter of a fact, bitch, I love it here!" I walked to the Unicor building across the street from the camp.

I was making close to three hundred and fifty dollars a month at the factory. Plus, I had another job cleaning Pen 2 Men's facility, the Warden's office along with the front lobby, plus SIS. I made almost a hundred a month there, so I couldn't trip. I was stacking my bread for when I was given that time to be free.

"How are you liking it there?" QBanga asked me.

"I am loving it here. I know how to load trucks and ship materials all over the world." I was the crew leader for my section. The men's Medium and Low made the materials and the women would receive it and ship it out.

"Bae, I am so proud of you. You didn't allow this bid to take you down, you took it down."

"Yea, I thought this shit was going to break me, but it's just making me stronger and better, for real." I rapped to QBanga before our phone call was cut off. He was definitely leaving an impression on me during this journey.

***

My home girl Lee was still riding. It had been close to two years and she was still standing beside me as I knocked days off the calendar. My kids were getting so big and grown.

"Mom, do you know where the dude that snitched on you lives?" My daughter asked me as soon as she answered the phone.

"Huh?" My daughter's statement caught me way off guard over the phone.

"The dude that told on you? Do you know where he is living?"

"No, why?"

"Because I have something that I want to say to him in person." The loyalty that she displayed for me, made my heart proud. She was my backbone during this journey. Her daily emails made my time so much better and easier.

"It's all good, baby."

"It's not all good. He could have kept his mouth shut, Mom."

"Yes, but he didn't, that's why I tell you all the time, loyalty over everything."

"I know, Mom. I know." Our conversation on the phone was always good, I was blessed to have the bond that we had.

She was big on loyalty, any time that my son Tamaine would snitch her out, she would snap. *"You know a snitch told on our mom, so you need to stop it, 'cause it doesn't look good on you at all."* I blamed myself daily for leaving them but I was mad blessed that their grandma was there to help me raise them. She was truly a blessing.

I heard the news about A-Town, and from time to time I would get a letter from him from his twin.

"Sis, how are you doing? I know you are keeping your head above water like the G that you are. Murda told me that you and him are no longer talking, that shit fucked me up 'cause y'all made the best couple there is. Anyway, I am good, just chilling, trying to take this shit back to court, but right now, I am on lock down for knocking a bitch ass officer the fuck out. The pussy tried to carry me so I let his ass have it. Know that I love you and you are the real definition of a last of a dying breed female.

Getting letters from him and Flow made my time smooth. I knew they were good and that's all that mattered.

"Jenkins!" Mr. Walker, our foreman yelled my name.

"Yo," I answered him.

"The message center needs you to report there."

"Huh?" Anytime the message center called, we were in some type of trouble. "Did they say why?"

"I know ya ass ain't scared."

"Nigga, fuck you!"

Mr. Walker was a cool ass officer, homie didn't treat us like inmates, but like humans. He wasn't on our backs like other officers were with their workers. As long as his floor with the materials were out, and the jobs were done well, he didn't give a fuck about what we did. I fucked with the nigga mad hard, 'cause he knew the struggle and the streets, he just made it out in time before it swallowed him.

"Shit, I was in the kitchen making shit bubble." He would rap, but I knew he really was about that shit back then.

As I made my way to the message center, Lannie stopped me. "They are calling you to the message center, Love."

"You know what for?"

"Naw."

"Thanks, though."

I tucked my shirt in 'cause I didn't know what the fuck was going on. And that was where the Warden's office was located. I pulled the front door open and stop at the station. "Y'all called Jenkins?" I asked the short, white officer on duty.

"Yes. The Warden's secretary wants you. You can go straight back there."

I cracked my knuckles before I opened the door, leading to the office. Once I got to the office, I knocked on the door.

"Come in." A voice spoke.

I opened the door and there were two officers in there along with the secretary. "My boss told me to come here."

"Your name?" I gave her my ID.

"Jenkins. Love Jenkins." I said my name.

She opened a black binder and told me to sign by my name. "It's legal mail, your counselor is not here today, so I am doing it." I signed my name and she opened the letter in front of me.

"I'm just making sure there is nothing in there."

"No problem."

Once she inspected the mail, she handed it over to me and I left the office. Instead of going back to work, I dashed to my unit, F2. Once I got inside my cube, I sat in the chair by the window and opened the mail.

Motion to Reduce Sentence

My name is Madeleine Lee, I was appointed to represent you from the fourth District for free. I am with the Public Defender's Office. I would like for you to look over this document attached to this letter. If you need to get in touch with me, my information is listed below. Thank you.

I couldn't even breath as I turned the next page. My hands were shaking so bad that I thought I was going to pass the fuck out. I started sweating profusely.

Comes now the Defendant Love Jenkins, by counsel, and respectfully moves this Honorable court, pursuant to 18 U.S.C. 3582(c) and the United States Guidelines Amendment 782 for an order reducing the term of her imprisonment from 180 months to 135 months.

My heart raced and I had to put the letter down and hold my chest. "What the hell?" I looked up at the ceiling as the tears dripped from my face. God was moving for me. "Lord, please, bless me."

The Supreme Court's recent decision in Hughes v. United States, 138 S.Ct. 1765(2018) makes Ms. Jenkins eligible for a reduction.

Tears dripped from my eyes as I held the paper out of the way. My palms were soaking wet as I held on the paper. My mind raced like a race track filled with horses.

1. Ms. Jenkins entered into a Plea Agreement under Federal Rule of Civil Procedure 11(c)(1)(c), (2) the district court was required to consider the Sentencing Guidelines before accepting the agreement, and (3) THERE is no clear demonstration the district court would have imposed the SAME sentence regardless of the sentencing guidelines. Ms. Jenkins' sentence should be reduced to 135 months.

Ms. Madeleine Lee was an angel. Her office was located out of Roanoke VA, where I got indictment at. As I read the rest of the document, she spoke on how I had filed for the reduction but I was denied twice. But since Hughes won the case against the United States, I was now eligible. I read the motion all the way to the end crying.

Ms. Jenkins' sentence of 180 months was within her sentencing guidelines range of 168-210 months. Applying the two-point base offense level reduction now, her guidelines range is 135-168 months incarceration. Ms. Jenkins requests that her sentence be reduced to 135 months.

I did the math in my head, if the judge changed my time to 135 months, then I would only have to do eleven and a few months instead of fifteen years. I was already down for a minute, and with the new law that Trump had just passed with the First Step Act, we were granted seven extra days. So instead of forty-seven good days, we got fifty-four per year. I was adding everything up so fast that my head started hurting.

"Damn a year halfway house, too." I said to myself. They were giving me a whole year in the halfway house due to all the years that I had done. "The year 2020," I whispered to myself as the tears ran freely. I was already claiming the news before it passed.

I stuffed the letter under my pillow and made a run for it to the multipurpose room to email my homie, Lee.

"Bitch, you are not about to believe this. I am not saying shit to anyone but you for right now. But this lawyer from VA is putting in for a reduction for me. OMG, bitch, and if I am adding it up right, I will be home in 2020, bitchhhhhhhhhhhh. I love you!"

I went back to work with a smile on my face as I prepared myself to touch the streets. "Muthafuckas better get ready!"

Chapter 36

Murdoc

I was sentenced altogether to five years but with good time and work release, I should be able to come home faster than expected. My ex-wife had moved on with her life, she stopped answering the calls once she found out that I was really messing with Love's best friend.

Snow made sure shit was perfect for me and even though she gained a few pounds the weight made her look extra thick. I had been trying to call her for the last hour nonstop, but nothing. I figured she was with her mother so I waited a few more hours to call again. Still nothing. Mail call came and when I didn't receive any mail from her, I knew something was wrong.

"What the fuck?" I said, joining the line to use the phone. The line was long as fuck, but if I didn't stay it would be longer later. So, I stayed. "Aye, can you hold my spot for me real quick? I am about to grab a book and come right back."

"Cool." And I ran to my bed to get my book. YaYo by S. Allen, was the shit. The nigga that wrote it had to have lived that life, that's how on point that shit was.

"Thanks for holding my spot, yo."

"No problem."

As I waited in line, I read. I couldn't put the book down. Lock Down Publications motto was right, *The Game is ours!* They dropped nothing but the best, from sex stories, to real live hood shit. On my list next was a series by Jamaica, Blood Stains of a Shotta, the three-part series.

By the time I got to the phone, I had four pages left before the book came to an end. I dialed Snow's number again and still no answer so I hit my little young nigga's line.

"Ayo, my nigga, what's good with you?" I asked as soon as he answered my call.

"Shit, fam, just cooling."

"Word?"

"Hell yeah, I tried reaching out to ya shorty but she hasn't picked up for me in four days, my nigga."

"What? Four days?" I knew I wasn't hearing my nigga correct. "She told me she spoke to you a day ago."

"Naw my nigga, not me, yo."

"What?"

"Yea, but I'ma spit some shit at you about shorty." I turned my back to the pod as I faced the wall listening. "She just had a baby."

His words hit me so hard that I dropped the book on the floor. "A baby?" I questioned my nigga.

"Yea, a baby." He repeated himself.

"What the fuck? She never told me she was pregnant." And she could not have been pregnant by me, because every time, I hit, I was strapped up.

"You ain't know, yo?"

"Fuck no, I didn't know."

"And word on the streets it's that nigga that just got forty-five years, baby."

"Huh?" My head was spinning hard as muthafucka.

"Yea, A-Town."

I hung the phone up on my nigga and picked the book up off the floor. Everything in front of my eyes were blurry. I held on to the wall as I walked to my bunk. "Murdoc, you good?" Kool, the white boy, asked me.

"Naw, I need you to find me something to ease this pain."

"Are you hurting?"

"Yea. See if you can get my cousin, Woody, to come see me. He got what I need."

I made it to my bed before I passed out. My heart ached, my head thumped, and my body felt numb. Woody arrived at my bed within seconds, "Fam, you good?"

"I need something to get high and knock me out for the night."

"Say less. I'll be back."

I climbed in my bed and stared up at the top bunk. All this time, Snow was playing me, she used me to the limit. There was nothing that I could do from in here, she had all my money, all the cars were in her name. I had to play it cool after I found out that she was the one that tipped the police off about my whereabouts because of the access that she had to everything that I had in my name.

"Fam, get up and pop this." He handed me a big ass pill and a cup of water. "I'll make sure you get up in the morning for breakfast." I popped the pill and handed him the cup back.

"Thanks." I laid my head back down and closed my eyes.

***

A day later, I was just coming out of a deep sleep. I was light headed as fuck but I stood to my feet as they counted us. "Count clear!"

"Fam, how are you feeling?" Woody walked over to my bed to check up on me.

"Shit, I don't even know, fam." I told him the truth.

"What's up?" He took a seat on the boxes that they gave us to put our commissary in. "Mane, this shit is crazy. You know the bitch that I was telling you about?" I paused to see if he remembered.

"Yea, the white joint, right?"

"Yea, that bitch!"

"What happened?" My cousin asked and I told her everything that I knew.

"Fuck! Eighty bands is a lot of bread, yo."

"Get me another one of those joints. I need to sleep till this bid is over with!"

Chapter 37

Qbanga

Fuck no, I never told Love about that shit that happened between me and shorty, and I damn sure wasn't about to tell her either. What she didn't know wouldn't kill her, but if she found out, I knew she would be sick. I had stepped my game all the way up, I connected myself with some Mexicans that were literally giving the work away for cheap. Twenty for a bird and that shit was cheap. All I had to do was have a spot for them to deliver it to, and I did. I would ship the money to them just like they shipped the product to me.

BankRoll reached out to me but the bond that we had was no longer there like it used it. When we were in the meetings for the organization, we kept it mutual. Me and Phat's bond got hella tight. My nigga was on my team along with Lil Bruh, another GD member. The three of us had our side of town on lock.

"You know BankRoll flexing with that nigga, Murda, hard?" Lil Bruh said as we were waiting on the packages to drop.

"Who's messing with who?" I glanced over at him before I looked in the back seat at Phat.

"BankRoll copping his work from the nigga from New York that they call Murda."

"Murda?" I gazed at Phat. "I told you that nigga wasn't loyal."

"You were right."

"What else do you know, Lil Bruh?" I listened as my little G put me up on the game. One thing about me, I would have never fucked with that nigga Murda if the shoe was on the other foot, but BankRoll didn't see that, he saw money and not loyalty.

"The postman here," Phat advised us. We watched as he pulled in front of the house. I had been waiting on these birds for a week now. So, seeing the mailman finally stopping here had a nigga ready to trap the fuck out and add this bag up.

He exited the mail van with a few boxes in his hand, he walked up to the door and knocked, when no one answered. He placed the boxes on the mat and scanned them before he walked back to his ride.

We waited for an hour in that same spot to make sure no one was going to do any surprise visits. Lil Bruh got out, as me and Phat circled the block to make sure shit was legit and a go. When he didn't see anything out of the ordinary, I hit Lil Bruh's phone.

"Pick the boxes up in ten seconds. Start counting now." I was pulling back up in front of the spot. Phat looked from the back seat at the back and I kept my eyes straight in front of me. Nothing moved which was great, my grandma would be home in a few hours. Everything was going according to the plan. The moment Lil Bruh sat in the car, I peeled off.

We made it back to my spot and I went to work, shorty was out of town with her family, so it gave me enough time and space to move around the crib freely without hearing her nagging like a fucking parrot.

"How much work do you need?" I asked Lil Bruh.

"Give me two, my G."

"Phat, what you want, my nigga?"

"Shit, I can handle whatever!" He said with confidence. I had ten birds in all, so I gave Phat four and kept four.

***

It's late as fuck and the only thing up with me was the stars and the moon. Niggas thought loyalty was just a one-way street, but with me, that shit always have to be a two-way road. What I gave out, I expected it back and more.

I found out from a reliable source where the nigga, Murda, was resting his head at.

"You sure it's only two of them there?"

"I'm telling you, it's just two of them there."

"So, BankRoll should be there tonight, for a fact?"

"For a fact. I can stamp it."

I parked my ride across the street from the barber shop and waited. For an hour or so nothing happened but I stayed in place. I refused to move or walk away. I was getting restless by the minute but I refused to allow myself to fail a task that I wanted to complete. Another ten minutes passed before I finally watched what was going down in front of my eyes. The nigga that I called my brother, my G, my homie, my best friend, was indeed fucking with this nigga, for real. My spirit crushed inside but the fuel of hate built up more and more for him.

The nigga that drove Murda that night to meet us on Federal Street opened the door. I was so glad that they had sensor lights around them 'cause if they didn't, I wouldn't have been able to see shit.

BankRoll dapped the nigga up and stepped inside. After all that shit that nigga spoke on homie, here he was copping from the nigga. Niggas words won't law these days, and in order for a muthafucka to see that, I had to show them. Loyalty over everything, even money.

It took BankRoll approximately twenty minutes before he exited the shop with a bag in his hands. My eyes never left his movements. When he pulled off, I pulled out in the opposite direction timing his way to his crib. I would get to his crib, first.

Once I got to his spot, I parked across the street. And waited.

A few minutes later, I watched the car lights turn on the block. Seeing him pulling into his driveway, I pulled the ski mask down my face. He never once looked behind him or around him as he got out of the car and started walking.

"Give me everything you got, nigga?" I placed the cold steel at the side of his head. The bag that he was carrying, dropped at his feet.

"You can have it all, yo. Just don't kill me."

"Empty ya pockets, yo." I jammed the burner deeper into his skull. He pulled out a knot and dropped it at his feet, also.

"I don't have anything else," he whined. "Please don't kill me," he begged.

"Get down on your knees, nigga. Fuck that lay the fuck down!"

Once he was flat on his stomach, I picked the wad of money and bag up. I have always been a stand-up nigga and I wasn't about to change now. I pulled my ski mask off my face and dropped it beside his head.

"Get up, nigga." I stood back as the nigga got on his feet. "Turn around."

"What the fuck?" he said, seeing my face from the porch light. "G?"

"You fucking with a nigga that I don't fuck with, nigga. Where is the loyalty in that, huh? I rode with you to smoke a nigga that was disloyal to you and this is how you pay me back? Fucking with a nigga that you know that don't fuck with me?" I never gave him a chance to say shit. "But since you fucking a nigga so tough, tell that nigga I took this shit and he can come see me!" I turned around and walked off, only stopping a few feet before I turned back around letting my hammer talk.

Blocka!

Chapter 38

Murda

I was present when Kandi had the baby, I took the scissors and cut the umbilical cord. She named the little mama, "My'Air." She was beautiful with curly jet-black hair that laid on her ears. She had dimples, a small nose and some big feet. The more and more I stare down at My'Air, I just couldn't see the resemblance with my other kids. She didn't look anything like me but more like her mom.

"I know you think that she is not your baby, but you can get a blood test, if you want?"

"Oh, I want a blood test, for sure." I said, getting up and looking at the baby in the cart. "Yea, I'ma need a blood test." I studied the baby girl's face. There wasn't a sign that she was mine.

"How long does a blood test take?" I turned around and looked at Kandi.

"A few days."

"Order one!" I said, walking out the door to find me a nurse so I could do a swab test. After I did that, I left. I needed to spend some time with my son.

The next few days, I took Marley up there to visit the hospital to check up on his mom and sister. He was so in awe with his sister, he couldn't stop looking at her, at one point, he was feeding her.

"Daddy, she is beautiful."

"Yes, she is!"

I dropped my son back off at his grandma and traveled back to the hospital. I brought Kandi some food to eat along with a few items for My'Air.

"You didn't have to get her anything," she said, rolling her eyes and I started thinking really hard, if she was mine, why not get her some things. Her comment made me look at her really hard.

An hour after I had been up there for Kandi to be released, the nurse walked in with a brown envelope. "I have the results here," I held the car seat in my hand as Kandi held a bag in hers.

My eyes never left My'Air, she was innocent, and also beautiful. If she was mine, I would love her more than my last breath. Nothing in the world would be able to ever come between our bond.

"Mr. Martin, you are…" I looked over at Kandi, 'cause I felt her eyes on me, "not the father." I looked down at baby girl and dropped my head further.

I heard Kandi gasp for air, but I didn't look back at her, no matter how much she told me that I was the father, I just felt different. I walked out the room with the baby in my hand. I got to the car and strapped her in before I pulled to the front of the building to pick Kandi up. I got out and even opened her door for her.

The ride on the way to the crib was silent beside me hearing Kandi crying softly. I reached my hand over and rubbed her leg. "I'll stand by you with her, anything you want and need for her, I got it for you. Don't be afraid to ask." She placed her hand on top of mine, but kept her face to the window. "I'll never treat her differently. Marley loves her."

Once I dropped Kandi off and made sure she was safe, I dropped a few bands on the table. "Kiss my son for me when ya mom drops him off." I leaned down and kissed the top of baby girl's head.

Love's words repeated over and over in my head as I hit the high. *"The girl you hurt the most, you are going to need her in the end. No matter how much money you have. A relationship is deeper than lust and money. Money can't buy you peace and happiness, but a female who fucks with you mentally, and emotionally is someone worth living for. At least you know if you lose it all, you don't have to question her loyalty. But don't break her heart, cause once you lose her, it's going to be hard to get her back. Nobody bounced back more than a woman who finally let hurt go!"*

"Fuck!" I punched the steering wheel thinking how my actions fucked my life up with Love.

Chapter 39

Love

Four months had flown by and I hadn't heard anything from the courts or the lawyer. I was still working and stacking my paper for my day. One thing I wasn't going to do was depend on a nigga, my mom told me that before she left me. If I had to get it from the mud, I was going to do just that. Nothing or no one was going to be able to stand in the road of me achieving everything that I wanted once this was over with.

I couldn't wait to spend that well needed time with my kids, they were all that I had, plus a few friends. I couldn't wait to see the faces of the ones that counted me out, that wished me back, ones that thought I was going to crumble. I couldn't wait to hold my sister, Flow, down, along with bruh, A-Town, plus a few ones that I met on this journey.

"Love Jenkins, report to the unit team in F2 middle!" My heart raced as I heard my name over the announcement speaker.

I got to the office and Ms. Lopez was sitting at her table, as her orderly, China, took the trash out. "Love, how are you doing?" China greeted me.

"Hey, boo, how are you doing?"

"Ready to go home," she said, walking past me, "I got fourteen days left."

"I know you happy as fuck, too."

"You already know." She disappeared from the small room.

"Love, take a seat."

I stepped inside the room and took the seat right across from her, with my hands entwined together. My right leg wouldn't stop jumping, I was nervous as fuck.

"I got an email regarding you today, but I didn't have a chance to call you because I have been so damn busy." She stood to her feet, putting her glasses on and pushing her monitor back so she could see.

I watched her click a few buttons then I heard the printer printing. She picked up the paper and handed it over to me. It was from the *UNITED STATES DISTRICT COURT for the Western District of Virginia.*

My name and case number were present, along with Madeleine Lee, the lawyer that filed the case.

The document read: IT IS ORDERED that the motion is ( )Denied- (X)Granted and the defendant's previously imposed sentence of imprisonment (as reflected in the last judgment issued) of 180 months is **REDUCED TO** 135 months.

_My heart dropped but the tears ran down my face. The scream that I wanted to release couldn't even come out. I stood to my feet, only to sit back down. Ms. Lopez watched me but I didn't say a word to her. I kept reading.

SENTENCE RELATIVE TO AMENDED GUIDELINE RANGE

(x) The reduced sentence is within the amended guideline range.

ADDITIONAL COMMENTS

*Defendant's term of imprisonment is reduced to 135 months, but not less than time served, as to each counts 1, 10, and 11, to be served concurrently. This sentence reduction is authorized by Hughes v. United States, 138 S. Ct 1765(2018) and United States Sentencing Guidelines Amendment 782.

"I have to start doing your halfway house paperwork. I need an address for you."

"You can use this one," I wrote down Lee's address. She said I was welcome to stay with her and get myself together, since I couldn't go back to Virginia because of that bitch made nigga that snitched on me and the whole city.

I emailed Lee and told her what was going on, I didn't call or tell my kids anything or QBanga. I was keeping it a secret, for sure.

A few days later, Ms. Lopez called me back in her office. "Your address is approved. And I am putting you in for a year halfway house."

"Thank you."

I raced back to my unit to call Lee. "Friend, your address is approved and my counselor said that she is putting me in for a year halfway house." I whispered into the phone.

"What?" She screamed at the top of her lungs. "My friend, you are on the way home, baby!" Lee stood by her words and even though she was a felon, she had got her life back in order and was off probation in no time. She did everything that she was supposed to do.

"You know all what I had to go through to get you here with me?"

"No, but I bet it was hell."

"It was, my friend, but it's all worth it. I am so happy for you and I can't wait to have you here with me."

***

I kept everything on the low from everyone, no one knew on the streets that I was about to touch but Lee.

Ms. Lopez called me a week later back into her office. "Your date is September 12th . I was able to get you a whole year halfway house time."

No matter how hard I was, I cried. My freedom was at the tip of my finger. I could literally taste freedom. I had nine months left to go.

Fucking out of the blue, the world was under watch with a thing call COVID19. People were getting sick and dying at a rapid speed. And the government was scared for it to hit the prison system, because of the space. If one person got it, they knew it would spread within the blink of an eye 'cause of the lack of space within the walls.

The Warden and her staff made rounds, with a lot of news.

"If you have a release date for this year, you could me leaving sooner than your release date."

Round of applause erupted around the units. People were going home sooner than they had expected. And I was one of them. Months flew by and people were starting to leave way before their time.

When Ms. Lopez called me into her office this time, I wasn't nervous or scared, a bitch was ready. "I got a new date for you, Love."

I sat in the chair and smiled. "Give it to me."

"June twenty-third."

"What?" I jumped up and down for like five minutes nonstop. "Yes, they're about to let a real bitch free!" I screamed on the inside.

A day later, I did my fingerprints. I didn't want any clothes sent in then people would know I was on my way out the door. I kept everything under lock and key. I called home and acted like nothing was going on. I mailed everything that I wanted to keep home to Lee.

She sent me an email days later and all I could do was cry; she was a real and true friend. Her loyalty was just like mine; we shared the same definition.

I was ready when they called my name to R and D, my close friends around me cried, but I assured them that they would hear from me. I was handed some cash from my account, a plane ticket and my blood pressure medicine. I didn't shed a tear; I had prayed for the day to come and I damn sure wasn't about to cry no more.

The camp driver that drove me, didn't talk, she drove and I took in the trip. My stomach didn't bubble or I wasn't nervous, I was just ready to get the hell away from Florida all the way together.

Once I got to the airport, I wished the driver the best on the remaining of her bid and walked right into the airport.

"Love!" I heard my name and when I saw Lee running towards me, I screamed. When she sent me the email that she was going to be here waiting on me, my heart poured out tears.

"Loyalty over everything!" She screamed as we hugged each other.

"I'm fucking *free!*"

"Yes, you are free." I pulled back from her embrace and looked into her eyes.

"Real bitches do real things!"

The End

Submission Guideline

Submit the first three chapters of your completed manuscript to ldpsubmissions@gmail.com, subject line: Your book's title. The manuscript must be in a .doc file and sent as an attachment. Document should be in Times New Roman, double spaced and in size 12 font. Also, provide your synopsis and full contact information. If sending multiple submissions, they must each be in a separate email.

Have a story but no way to send it electronically? You can still submit to LDP/Ca$h Presents. Send in the first three chapters, written or typed, of your completed manuscript to:

LDP: Submissions Dept
Po Box 944
Stockbridge, Ga 30281

DO NOT send original manuscript. Must be a duplicate.

Provide your synopsis and a cover letter containing your full contact information.

Thanks for considering LDP and Ca$h Presents.

BOW DOWN TO MY GANGSTA

By **Ca$h**

TORN BETWEEN TWO

By **Coffee**

THE STREETS STAINED MY SOUL **II**

By **Marcellus Allen**

BLOOD OF A BOSS **VI**

SHADOWS OF THE GAME II

By **Askari**

LOYAL TO THE GAME **IV**

By **T.J. & Jelissa**

IF LOVING YOU IS WRONG… **III**

By **Jelissa**

TRUE SAVAGE **VIII**

MIDNIGHT CARTEL III

DOPE BOY MAGIC IV

CITY OF KINGZ II

By **Chris Green**

BLAST FOR ME **III**

A SAVAGE DOPEBOY III

CUTTHROAT MAFIA III

DUFFLE BAG CARTEL VI

By **Ghost**

A HUSTLER'S DECEIT III

KILL ZONE **II**

BAE BELONGS TO ME III

A DOPE BOY'S QUEEN III

By **Aryanna**

Jamaica

COKE KINGS V

KING OF THE TRAP II

By **T.J. Edwards**

GORILLAZ IN THE BAY V

3X KRAZY II

De'Kari

THE STREETS ARE CALLING II

Duquie Wilson

KINGPIN KILLAZ IV

STREET KINGS III

PAID IN BLOOD III

CARTEL KILLAZ IV

DOPE GODS III

Hood Rich

SINS OF A HUSTLA II

ASAD

KINGZ OF THE GAME VI

Playa Ray

SLAUGHTER GANG IV

RUTHLESS HEART IV

By Willie Slaughter

THE HEART OF A SAVAGE III

By Jibril Williams

FUK SHYT II

By Blakk Diamond

TRAP QUEEN

By Troublesome

YAYO V

GHOST MOB

Stilloan Robinson

Last of a Dying Breed 2

KINGPIN DREAMS III

By Paper Boi Rari

CREAM II

By Yolanda Moore

SON OF A DOPE FIEND III

By Renta

FOREVER GANGSTA II

GLOCKS ON SATIN SHEETS III

By Adrian Dulan

LOYALTY AIN'T PROMISED III

By Keith Williams

THE PRICE YOU PAY FOR LOVE II

By Destiny Skai

CONFESSIONS OF A GANGSTA III

By Nicholas Lock

I'M NOTHING WITHOUT HIS LOVE II

SINS OF A THUG II

By Monet Dragun

LIFE OF A SAVAGE IV

MURDA SEASON IV

GANGLAND CARTEL III

CHI'RAQ GANGSTAS II

By **Romell Tukes**

QUIET MONEY IV

THUG LIFE II

EXTENDED CLIP II

By **Trai'Quan**

THE STREETS MADE ME III

By **Larry D. Wright**

IF YOU CROSS ME ONCE II

Jamaica

ANGEL III

By **Anthony Fields**

FRIEND OR FOE III

By **Mimi**

SAVAGE STORMS II

By **Meesha**

BLOOD ON THE MONEY III

By J-Blunt

THE STREETS WILL NEVER CLOSE II

By K'ajji

NIGHTMARES OF A HUSTLA III

By King Dream

THE WIFEY I USED TO BE II

By Nicole Goosby

IN THE ARM OF HIS BOSS

By Jamila

MONEY, MURDER & MEMORIES II

Malik D. Rice

CONCRETE KILLAZ II

By Kingpen

HARD AND RUTHLESS II

By Von Wiley Hall

Available Now

RESTRAINING ORDER **I & II**
By **CA$H & Coffee**
LOVE KNOWS NO BOUNDARIES **I II & III**
By **Coffee**
RAISED AS A GOON I, II, III & IV
BRED BY THE SLUMS I, II, III
BLAST FOR ME I & II
ROTTEN TO THE CORE I II III
A BRONX TALE I, II, III
DUFFLE BAG CARTEL I II III IV V
HEARTLESS GOON I II III IV
A SAVAGE DOPEBOY I II
HEARTLESS GOON I II III
DRUG LORDS I II III
CUTTHROAT MAFIA I II
By **Ghost**
LAY IT DOWN **I & II**
LAST OF A DYING BREED I II
BLOOD STAINS OF A SHOTTA I & II III
By **Jamaica**
LOYAL TO THE GAME I II III
LIFE OF SIN I, II III
By **TJ & Jelissa**
BLOODY COMMAS I & II
SKI MASK CARTEL I II & III
KING OF NEW YORK I II,III IV V
RISE TO POWER I II III
COKE KINGS I II III IV
BORN HEARTLESS I II III IV
KING OF THE TRAP

Jamaica

By **T.J. Edwards**
IF LOVING HIM IS WRONG…I & II
LOVE ME EVEN WHEN IT HURTS I II III
By **Jelissa**
WHEN THE STREETS CLAP BACK I & II III
THE HEART OF A SAVAGE I II
By **Jibril Williams**
A DISTINGUISHED THUG STOLE MY HEART I II & III
LOVE SHOULDN'T HURT I II III IV
RENEGADE BOYS I II III IV
PAID IN KARMA I II III
SAVAGE STORMS
By **Meesha**
A GANGSTER'S CODE I &, II III
A GANGSTER'S SYN I II III
THE SAVAGE LIFE I II III
CHAINED TO THE STREETS I II III
BLOOD ON THE MONEY I II
By **J-Blunt**
PUSH IT TO THE LIMIT
By **Bre' Hayes**
BLOOD OF A BOSS **I, II, III, IV, V**
SHADOWS OF THE GAME
By **Askari**
THE STREETS BLEED MURDER **I, II & III**
THE HEART OF A GANGSTA I II& III
By **Jerry Jackson**
CUM FOR ME I II III IV V VI
An **LDP Erotica Collaboration**
BRIDE OF A HUSTLA **I II & II**

210

THE FETTI GIRLS **I, II& III**

CORRUPTED BY A GANGSTA I, II III, IV

BLINDED BY HIS LOVE

THE PRICE YOU PAY FOR LOVE

DOPE GIRL MAGIC I II III

By **Destiny Skai**

WHEN A GOOD GIRL GOES BAD

By **Adrienne**

THE COST OF LOYALTY I II III

By Kweli

A GANGSTER'S REVENGE **I II III & IV**

THE BOSS MAN'S DAUGHTERS I II III IV V

A SAVAGE LOVE **I & II**

BAE BELONGS TO ME I II

A HUSTLER'S DECEIT I, II, III

WHAT BAD BITCHES DO I, II, III

SOUL OF A MONSTER I II III

KILL ZONE

A DOPE BOY'S QUEEN I II

By **Aryanna**

A KINGPIN'S AMBITON

A KINGPIN'S AMBITION **II**

I MURDER FOR THE DOUGH

By **Ambitious**

TRUE SAVAGE I II III IV V VI VII

DOPE BOY MAGIC I, II, III

MIDNIGHT CARTEL I II

CITY OF KINGZ

By **Chris Green**

A DOPEBOY'S PRAYER

Jamaica

By **Eddie "Wolf" Lee**
THE KING CARTEL **I, II & III**
By **Frank Gresham**
THESE NIGGAS AIN'T LOYAL **I, II & III**
By **Nikki Tee**
GANGSTA SHYT **I II &III**
By **CATO**
THE ULTIMATE BETRAYAL
By **Phoenix**
BOSS'N UP **I , II & III**
By **Royal Nicole**
I LOVE YOU TO DEATH
By Destiny J
I RIDE FOR MY HITTA
I STILL RIDE FOR MY HITTA
By **Misty Holt**
LOVE & CHASIN' PAPER
By **Qay Crockett**
TO DIE IN VAIN
SINS OF A HUSTLA
By **ASAD**
BROOKLYN HUSTLAZ
By **Boogsy Morina**
BROOKLYN ON LOCK I & II
By **Sonovia**
GANGSTA CITY
By **Teddy Duke**
A DRUG KING AND HIS DIAMOND I & II III
A DOPEMAN'S RICHES
HER MAN, MINE'S TOO I, II

CASH MONEY HO'S

THE WIFEY I USED TO BE

By Nicole Goosby

TRAPHOUSE KING **I II & III**

KINGPIN KILLAZ I II III

STREET KINGS I II

PAID IN BLOOD **I II**

CARTEL KILLAZ I II III

DOPE GODS I II

By **Hood Rich**

LIPSTICK KILLAH **I, II, III**

CRIME OF PASSION I II & III

FRIEND OR FOE I II

By **Mimi**

STEADY MOBBN' **I, II, III**

THE STREETS STAINED MY SOUL

By **Marcellus Allen**

WHO SHOT YA **I, II, III**

SON OF A DOPE FIEND I II

Renta

GORILLAZ IN THE BAY **I II III IV**

TEARS OF A GANGSTA I II

3X KRAZY

DE'KARI

TRIGGADALE I II III

Elijah R. Freeman

GOD BLESS THE TRAPPERS I, II, III

THESE SCANDALOUS STREETS I, II, III

FEAR MY GANGSTA I, II, III IV, V

THESE STREETS DON'T LOVE NOBODY I, II

Jamaica

BURY ME A G I, II, III, IV, V

A GANGSTA'S EMPIRE I, II, III, IV

THE DOPEMAN'S BODYGAURD I II

THE REALEST KILLAZ I II III

Tranay Adams

THE STREETS ARE CALLING

Duquie Wilson

MARRIED TO A BOSS... I II III

By Destiny Skai & Chris Green

KINGZ OF THE GAME I II III IV V

Playa Ray

SLAUGHTER GANG I II III

RUTHLESS HEART I II III

By Willie Slaughter

FUK SHYT

By Blakk Diamond

DON'T F#CK WITH MY HEART I II

By Linnea

ADDICTED TO THE DRAMA I II III

IN THE ARM OF HIS BOSS II

By Jamila

YAYO I II III IV

A SHOOTER'S AMBITION I II

By S. Allen

TRAP GOD I II III

By Troublesome

FOREVER GANGSTA

GLOCKS ON SATIN SHEETS I II

By Adrian Dulan

TOE TAGZ I II III

By Ah'Million
KINGPIN DREAMS I II
By Paper Boi Rari
CONFESSIONS OF A GANGSTA I II
By Nicholas Lock
I'M NOTHING WITHOUT HIS LOVE
SINS OF A THUG
By Monet Dragun
CAUGHT UP IN THE LIFE I II III
By Robert Baptiste
NEW TO MONEY, MURDER & MEMORIES
THE GAME I II III
By **Malik D. Rice**
LIFE OF A SAVAGE I II III
A GANGSTA'S QUR'AN I II III
MURDA SEASON I II III
GANGLAND CARTEL I II
CHI'RAQ GANGSTAS
By **Romell Tukes**
LOYALTY AIN'T PROMISED I II
By Keith Williams
QUIET MONEY I II III
THUG LIFE
EXTENDED CLIP
By **Trai'Quan**
THE STREETS MADE ME I II
By **Larry D. Wright**
THE ULTIMATE SACRIFICE I, II, III, IV, V, VI
KHADIFI
IF YOU CROSS ME ONCE

Jamaica

ANGEL I II
By **Anthony Fields**
THE LIFE OF A HOOD STAR
By **Ca$h & Rashia Wilson**
THE STREETS WILL NEVER CLOSE
By **K'ajji**
CREAM
By **Yolanda Moore**
NIGHTMARES OF A HUSTLA I II
By **King Dream**
CONCRETE KILLAZ
By **Kingpen**
HARD AND RUTHLESS
By **Von Wiley Hall**

BOOKS BY LDP'S CEO, CA$H

TRUST IN NO MAN

TRUST IN NO MAN 2

TRUST IN NO MAN 3

BONDED BY BLOOD

SHORTY GOT A THUG

THUGS CRY

THUGS CRY 2

THUGS CRY 3

TRUST NO BITCH

TRUST NO BITCH 2

TRUST NO BITCH 3

TIL MY CASKET DROPS

RESTRAINING ORDER

RESTRAINING ORDER 2

IN LOVE WITH A CONVICT

LIFE OF A HOOD STAR

Jamaica

www.ingramcontent.com/pod-product-compliance
Lightning Source LLC
Chambersburg PA
CBHW070456260626
47161CB00004B/1333